Return to Paradise Cove

Return to Paradise Cove

ROBERTA THOMAS

AVALON BOOKS
THOMAS BOUREGY AND COMPANY, INC.
401 LAFAYETTE STREET
NEW YORK, NEW YORK 10003

Library of Congress Catalog Card Number: 89-61477
ISBN 0-8034-8767-3

PRINTED IN THE UNITED STATES OF AMERICA
BY HADDON CRAFTSMEN, SCRANTON, PENNSYLVANIA

To Mark, Terry, and Todd

With love, all things become possible.

Chapter One

As a gentle sea breeze caressed her long, tawny hair and the noonday sun shone brightly, Julie Hartwell put on her aviator sunglasses and pushed off from shore in *Summer's Delight,* her small sailboat. She intended to take full advantage of the fine weather for sailing. The route through the channel, separating the mainland from Braddock's Island, was familiar to her, since she'd taken it countless times during past summers. Now once again she listened to the roar of the incoming tide and the cries of the circling gulls.

Out on the bay, her small craft glided across the shimmering surface, the boat's billowing sail eagerly embracing the wind. Intoxicated by the freshness of the salt air and lulled by the rays of the sun, she stretched out on the decking and closed her eyes, relaxing her grip on the tiller. Soon she found herself thinking again about Senator Roger Whitman, her employer in Washington, D.C.

Her father had introduced her to the tall, distinguished-looking politician, whose hair and mustache were touched with gray. Roger had been spending the weekend at her father's summer home, The Gull's Way. She had just earned her degree in government and had been impressed by his eloquence on the issues of poverty, homelessness, and the dangers of nuclear war. Brimming with youthful idealism, she had been eager to help him save the world. When he had suggested that she come to work as a staff aide in his office, she had promptly accepted his offer.

But once she was in Washington, her initial excitement over being at the center of national power soon gave way to the reality of her daily routine as a staff aide. Despite his hectic schedule, however, whenever Roger was in the office, he always found time to chat with her, and he even requested her presence at events after normal working hours. At first Julie had felt flattered, but soon Roger's romantic interest in her had become obvious. Despite her own warm regard for him, Julie had not responded. Roger was already engaged to Tracy Brooks, a wealthy socialite whose kindness and warmth had earned Julie's friendship and respect.

This vacation was a welcome opportunity for Julie to return to her favorite summer haunt, Paradise Cove, and to think seriously about her relationship with the senator. But the time had passed quickly, and though this was her last day in the seaside community, she still had conflicting emotions about Roger.

"Hey, watch out!" she heard someone yell. The shouted warning shattered her reverie and brought her bolt upright—too late to prevent the bow of her sailboat from hitting the dinghy broadside and hurling both her and its occupant into the water.

"Are you okay?" she asked the young man treading water nearby as she clung to the side of the overturned sailboat.

"Yes, but no thanks to you," he icily replied.

"Your rowboat looks fine," she said, trying to make the best of the embarrassing situation. "But my sailboat has a hairline crack in the hull."

"That serves you right," he told her, pushing his dark, wet hair back from his hazel eyes. "I suggest you change its name from *Summer's Delight* to *Summer's Disaster.*"

"I'm sorry about the accident," she said sharply, irritated by his gibe. "Do you have to be so rude?"

"Look, lady," he said sarcastically, "because of your negligence I've narrowly escaped serious injury. I've also lost a hundred-dollar rod and reel—not to mention an expensive tackle box." Sounding less angry, he added, "I'll help you upend your happy little craft if you'll help me track down my oars."

With a few short strokes he swam to her side. Together they righted her sailboat, and Julie quickly slithered on board. The sight of her supple body in a clinging blue halter and pink shorts abruptly ended his complaining.

"What are you waiting for?" she asked, motioning him to join her.

Still gazing at her approvingly, he shook his head.

"I refuse to let you drown—much as I might enjoy watching it happen," she said impatiently.

Her sarcasm broke the spell. "I have no intention of giving you that satisfaction," he replied curtly. "I'll turn the bow of my skiff toward the island so the current will carry me there. If you'll get my oars before they float across the Atlantic, I'll be grateful." He swam back to his dinghy and forced it around so that its bow faced the island. Soon the current, just as he had predicted, was sweeping him and the dinghy toward the island.

Meanwhile the fuming Julie was tempted to abandon him and set sail for the mainland. But she bit her tongue and retrieved the oars. By the time she reached the island, he had already made his way onshore and was struggling to turn over the rowboat and drain it of water. Reluctantly she got out of her sailboat and went to his aid. "Stop playing Superman and let me give you a hand," she said, unable to resist the gibe.

His glare silenced her. Together they managed to lift the boat's gunwale and empty the water. Afterward he slumped down breathlessly and said, "You really ought to learn how to control your sailboat."

Stung by the mild rebuke in his voice, she retorted, "You should have blown your whistle to warn me!"

He shook his head in disbelief. "I was minding my own business, trying to do some fishing, when you slammed into my skiff, almost drowning me. Now you blame me."

Ignoring his words, she went on, "You didn't have a whistle or a flotation device—both of which are required by state law."

"Aye, aye, sir," he said with a mock salute. "Now I suppose you'll have me walk the plank."

"Besides," she continued, "you shouldn't have been fishing in a narrow channel used constantly by sailboats from the yacht club."

"Since when is it a crime to fish anywhere on this bay?" he demanded, his voice rising. "I've been catching some good flounder in that spot."

Satisfied she had made her point, she turned to leave.

"Where do you think you're going?" he asked.

"As far away from you as possible."

He was on his feet, following her. "I want your name and address," he told her.

"I don't care what you want," she said, walking on.

"You're going to pay me for that lost rod and reel."

She didn't reply, speechless at the sight of her sailboat floating off the tip of the island. Throwing herself down on the sand, she exclaimed, "*Now* see what you've done!"

"Blaming me has become a way of life with you," he said. Glancing at the drifting boat, he added, "Personally I think the fates are punishing you."

Her face reddened in fury. "You're the rudest man I've ever met!"

"You wouldn't win any medals for manners, either!" he retorted.

She got up and stalked along the water's edge, biting her bottom lip as *Summer's Delight* floated farther away.

"If you asked me politely, I might row out and get it for you," he said more gently.

She whirled around. "Don't do me any favors!" Unwilling to let him see how unhappy she was, she turned away and stared furiously in the opposite direction. Out of the corner of her eye she saw him rowing with powerful strokes to overtake the sailboat. She sighed with relief when he caught up with it.

Soon he returned with the sailboat in tow. Determined to ignore him, she was sitting on a rock with her knees drawn up to her chin. Although she knew the accident was her fault, she resented his attempt to humiliate her. His sharp tongue made her think of Roger Whitman, but this stranger totally lacked the senator's poise and polish. No doubt this infuriating man would swagger up to her now with a lecture on the importance of responsibility. *Just let him try,* she thought angrily. She was ready to answer his insolence with some of her own.

As the bow of his dinghy hit the shore, he leaped onto the white sand in one smooth motion. He had taken off his wet T-shirt and now wore only cutoff denims. She stole glances at the muscles in his broad shoulders and taut calves, which were straining as he hauled her sailboat onto the beach. Grudgingly she admitted to herself that under different circumstances she would have found him attractive.

Turning to her, he said, "I've brought you a peace offering."

"Don't expect me to fall down and kiss your feet," she said, rising from her perch on the rock.

"I'm much more democratic than that. I'll

settle for a simple thank you." For the first time he smiled at her.

Refusing to be won over, she said, "That's more than you deserve after your behavior to me."

A look of frustration replaced his smile. "I admit that I lost my temper earlier," he said.

"Maybe there's some hope for you after all." She moved past him to reclaim her boat. "At least you know when you've acted badly."

"What did you expect after running into me?"

Sensing she had him on the defensive, she continued triumphantly, "I expected you to behave like a decent human being but apparently that was hoping for the impossible."

He observed her trying without success to push the sailboat back into the water, and he came over to help. As the sailboat slid into the water, she hopped aboard.

"Can't we at least part on friendly terms?" he asked, watching her hoist the sail.

"All I want is a parting," she replied as the boat edged away from him.

With a shrug of resignation he climbed into the dinghy and began rowing away from the island. Suddenly Julie wheeled the sailboat around and made a pass across his bow. "My name's Julie Hartwell. Send the bill for your rod and reel to me at Lantern Lane," she called. "I'll be glad to reimburse you for your lost toys." Then she sailed toward the mainland.

Her anger was still visible when she entered The Gull's Way, her father's rambling summer home. The slamming of the door startled her father, who was poring over the financial pages of the newspaper. "What's the matter?" he asked, looking up at her over his bifocals.

"I had an accident with my sailboat; the hull's cracked," she blurted out, slumping down onto a rattan sofa.

"That can be easily repaired," he said, putting his paper aside. "But are you okay?" he asked with concern.

"Yes," she assured him, running a hand through her tousled hair, "except that my pride is wounded."

"Now, that will be more difficult to fix," he said, looking relieved.

"It was my fault," she admitted. "I ran into some fisherman's rowboat. But I wasn't prepared to deal with his nastiness."

"You could hardly have expected him to praise you," he observed.

"No, but I've never met such a rude person."

"The quality of the summer people visiting Paradise Cove isn't what it used to be," he said consolingly.

"The nerve of him," Julie muttered, still smarting over the encounter.

"I think you should try to get some rest,"

her father said, "since you're leaving for Washington tomorrow morning." He couldn't hide his sadness over her impending departure.

"I know," she said wistfully.

"You don't sound thrilled about going back."

"I'm not." She sighed. "This past year I've really missed Paradise Cove."

"Why don't you stay?"

She heard the note of pleading in his voice. From the beginning he had opposed her decision to work in Washington. Even now she could remember the pained look on his face when the senator had offered her the staff job. Afterward her father had done his best to persuade her not to take it.

Since the death of his wife, Julie's father had become doting and protective—sometimes to the point of smothering Julie with fatherly love. As much as she cared for him, she needed to put more distance between them. If nothing else, the job in Washington had allowed her to do exactly that. "I've made a commitment to remain there for a year," she reminded him matter-of-factly. "I've got only a few months to go."

For a long time he studied her before saying, "I'm getting the impression Roger has more than a professional interest in you."

"Oh, I wouldn't say that," she said lightly, sorry she had to lie to him.

Disregarding her denial, he said, "I don't feel he'd make a good husband for you."

His suggestion that she and Roger were linked romantically brought a crimson blush to her face. Although she had always sensed that he had little regard for the senator, she knew that her father was compelled to hold his tongue, since he was slated to become the next chief executive officer of Acme Electronics, a company heavily dependent upon the government contracts that Roger Whitman could supply. Given her father's honesty, Julie knew his restraint didn't come easy. Now, for the first time, he had revealed his true feelings about the politician.

"I think you're jumping to conclusions," she managed to reply. "Roger is engaged to someone else."

"Such a minor detail would never stop Roger. Once he sets his mind on something, he goes after it," her father said, adding, "and he usually gets it."

With a shrug, she said, "Besides, he may not be my type."

"What kind of man is your type?" he asked in surprise.

"I'm not sure. But when Mr. Right comes along, I'll recognize him. Don't bells ring and sparks fly?" she asked teasingly.

"If that's true," he replied with a twinkle in his eye, "you've already met him."

"What do you mean?" she said, getting up.

"I got the impression that sparks flew between you and that fellow you just ran into out on the bay."

"I'm afraid those were the wrong kind of sparks," she replied tersely as she retreated to her bedroom to shower and prepare for the long drive back to Washington in the morning.

Later that night she lay in bed, thinking about her father's last words. Out on the bay, sparks certainly had flown between her and the insolent stranger. Unfortunately the fire had been fueled by conflict, not love. As she drifted off to sleep, she wondered just what the other kind might feel like.

Chapter Two

From the rear of the hall, Julie could see that Roger Whitman was enjoying his role as keynote speaker at the annual meeting of defense contractors. To his delight they kept interrupting him with outbursts of applause. As he stood confidently before the microphone in his custom-made, gray three-piece suit, the thought crossed her mind that he might have just stepped out of a clothing advertisement in some sophisticated men's magazine. A tiepin in the likeness of the American flag, a red handkerchief protruding from the pocket of his suit coat, his Phi Beta Kappa key—all these accessories enhanced his aura of competence.

He ended his speech with a flourish. "Eternal vigilance is still the price of freedom," he proclaimed, his voice booming off the walls, "and I can assure you that as an elected senator of this vast and bountiful land, I'll vigorously support a defense program that is second to none in the world."

Long afterward he lingered at center stage, savoring the adulation of the audience. Finally the convention marshals escorted him down. As he slowly made his way up the main aisle, he stopped to shake all available hands, giving an extra squeeze of cordiality to those who had contributed to his last campaign.

Julie, who had been listening with rapt attention, marveled at the ease with which the words and phrases rolled off his tongue. Even more surprising was the eagerness of his listeners to seize upon them. When at last he reached her side, he gave her a conspiratorial wink, whispering, "I want you to join me in the lounge for a drink."

With a glance at her watch she protested, "Oh, Roger, it's getting late. I really should be going."

"Your duties this evening aren't over," he informed her, his green eyes betraying an inner ardor. "It's true that tonight you've added a touch of class to my mundane senatorial routine, but you still need to critique my speech. What better way than over liquid refreshment?"

She always had trouble saying no to him and tonight was no exception. "Okay," she said with a sigh of resignation, "but just for a little while."

Already he had her by the arm and was leading her out of the hall.

Over cocktails in a dimly lit corner of the hotel lounge, he settled back in his chair and asked, "How was my delivery tonight?"

From the confident tone of his voice she felt he already knew the answer. At times his vanity and sense of self-importance annoyed her, but she was giving an honest opinion as she replied, "That was a stellar performance."

"Yes, I was in rare form," he said smugly.

"Many in the audience expressed a desire to help you in your reelection campaign," she said matter-of-factly.

"I'll soon be asking them to dig deeply into their pockets," he replied with a cynical laugh.

Since she failed to see the humor in his last remark, Julie didn't even smile. Leaning across the table, Roger became more serious. "I want to commend you for your research efforts on the defense issue," he said. "It was a first-rate job. I couldn't have delivered the speech without your help."

"Thanks," she replied, pleased that he appreciated her work.

Her turquoise satin dress shimmered beneath a revolving strobe light, and Roger eyed her appreciatively. "You're an unusual person," he whispered.

"I trust that's meant as a compliment," she said, shifting uneasily under his scrutiny.

"Yes, of course," he said, his gaze sweeping over her. "Your intelligence is exceeded only by your beauty."

"Careful, or I might accuse you of being chauvinistic," she lightly warned him.

"I'm simply being human," he assured her. "Ever since arriving here in Washington, you've been a tremendous help to me. Like strawberries and whipped cream, we go well together."

"You seem to have done nicely on your own," she managed to reply.

"With the right partner I could do even better."

Avoiding his gaze, she tried to dismiss his words with a shrug. After what seemed an eternity, he asked, "Do you know my name's being bandied about as a possible presidential candidate?"

"That doesn't really surprise me." She was well aware of the enormity of his personal ambitions.

Slowly his hand slid across the table to clasp hers. The amorous gesture caught her off guard, and she blurted out, "I'm sure Tracy Brooks will be of great help to you in achieving your goals."

He released his grip and leaned back in his chair. "I won't deny that Tracy and I have been close, but appearances can be deceiving. I'm going to tell you something I've never shared with anyone else." He chose his words with great care. "Tracy's a wonderful person and I certainly wouldn't do anything to hurt her, but I think we're both beginning to have second thoughts about marriage."

"Oh?" She raised an eyebrow questioningly.

"Her father was responsible for launching my political career, and I'll always be indebted to him." He smoothed out the edges of his mustache. "When he died in the midst of my senatorial campaign, Tracy assumed control of the family investment business. To my pleasant surprise, she continued to support my candidacy both in word and deed."

Julie shifted her weight, feeling like a constituent listening to one of his campaign speeches.

"We started dating, and our engagement eventually followed. Ever since my election victory, the media's been talking about our impending marriage. Well, I'm telling you it's not going to happen." He studied her, trying to measure her reaction to his words.

Like everyone else on his staff, Julie knew that the Brooks family had raised large sums of money for Roger's campaign. Despite her wealth Tracy had remained unspoiled. Her manner and appearance certainly didn't fit the stereotype of the typical socialite. At times she'd even come to Roger's office to lend a helping hand. Julie had come to like and respect the plump, freckle-faced woman with the laughing eyes and ready smile.

"Right now I'm interested in someone else," Roger said, intruding upon her thoughts.

Again she chose not to respond to his hidden meaning.

"She's an attractive blonde with eyes bluer than the seas, and a smile that would melt a polar ice cap." His attempt at poetic banter made Julie blush, and she didn't see his smile quickly vanish. "Here comes trouble," he muttered.

She looked up to see a tall, ruggedly built man with dark, wavy hair and hazel eyes standing in front of their table. He looked vaguely familiar but she couldn't place his face. "I heard your speech tonight," the stranger said in a voice heavy with sarcasm.

"You don't sound impressed, Baxter," Roger replied coolly.

"Frankly, I wasn't. I don't know of anyone in the Senate who isn't in favor of a strong defense."

Roger stiffened at his challenge. "Why must you always attack my patriotism?"

"Because patriotism is still the last refuge of a scoundrel," the young man responded sharply.

Julie could sense that he enjoyed sparring with the senator and, she found to her surprise, that he could more than hold his own. He was certainly a refreshing change from the back-slappers and servile flatterers who usually surrounded Roger.

Offended by his words, Roger shot back, "You know darn well you've never had one good thing to say about me."

"On the contrary, I approve of your taste in women." For the first time his eyes turned to her. "Aren't you Julie Hartwell?"

She had been listening intently to the exchange of words between them, and now his casual reference to her by name startled her. "Yes," she managed to reply, "but I don't believe we've met."

"You mean you've forgotten already?" His face broke out into an infectious smile.

"I'm afraid so," she said, embarrassed that she could fail to remember someone so good-looking.

"There's very little Mr. Baxter forgets, I can assure you," Roger muttered.

Ignoring Roger's jibe, he persisted, "Surely you recall the attempted homicide?"

"What are you talking about?" Roger's peevish query saved Julie from asking the same question.

"Do you still have the weapon?" His eyes, twinkling in amusement, remained on her. "I believe it was a sailboat."

"Oh, no!" she gasped. She was thankful the

dimness of the lounge hid her blush as she now vividly recalled their encounter out on the bay.

Roger, a pained expression on his face, was toying with his mustache and fidgeting in his chair. Julie didn't know whether his distress was the result of his contempt for the young intruder or petulance at not being the center of the conversation. Remembering the stranger's rudeness at the time of the boat accident, she rallied to Roger's defense by saying, "I can see your manners still haven't improved."

He glared at her but said nothing.

Her remark galvanized Roger into action. Rising, he said gruffly, "If you'll excuse us, Baxter, we have to be going. We both have busy schedules tomorrow."

"It's nice to know the taxpayers are getting their money's worth," the young man said with mock sincerity. As Julie arose he extended his hand, which she took hesitantly. "Allow me to introduce myself. Ned Baxter's the name. I'm sorry I didn't make a more positive impression on you at our last meeting."

To show he laid sole claim to her affections, Roger slipped an arm around Julie's slender waist and began to lead her out of the lounge. Glancing back at Ned Baxter, she said, "You never did send me a bill for your rod and reel."

"I saw no reason for you to pay for my toys," Ned said, flashing her an irresistible grin.

The meaning in his words didn't es
and suddenly she felt a sense of shame
parting shot to him the day of the boat acci-
dent. But Roger whisked her away before she could decide upon a suitable response.

Out in the parking lot, he said fretfully, "I didn't know you two had met."

"I wouldn't exactly call it a meeting," she replied matter-of-factly. "It was more of a chance encounter."

His face darkened. "What's going on between you two?" he demanded, his lips thinning in irritation.

Surprised by his sudden display of jealousy, she stared at him before replying, "Last summer my sailboat accidentally hit his rowboat, and we both ended up in the water."

"That's all?" He surveyed her suspiciously.

"Yes," she replied curtly.

His eyes brightened. Sensing her displeasure at his outburst, he murmured, "Forgive me, I had no right to speak to you that way."

Her annoyance at his temper tantrum yielded to her interest in the other man. "Who is he?" she asked.

"A columnist for the *Banner*—and not a good one," he said, unable to resist a verbal swipe at his adversary.

"But he's so young," she observed.

"During his senior year in college he did an internship with the newspaper, and he came up with the idea for a politically oriented gossip column entitled 'Washington Whispers.' "

"I see," she murmured, unable to repress a grudging admiration for his creativity.

"It made him an overnight sensation in the capital, so when he graduated, the editor hired him. Now rumor has it that he's not happy there and may resign." In a voice dripping with sarcasm, Roger added, "Personally, I can't wait."

"Why don't you like him?" she asked, opening the door to her car.

"Because he's ruined a perfectly wonderful hour with you," Roger said, taking her in his arms and kissing her.

Outside the office Roger had made no secret of his fondness for her, nor could she deny a certain fascination with the powerful, persuasive senator. Despite Roger's engagement to Tracy, Julie had known that this first kiss was inevitable. In a perverse way, she had even looked forward to it.

But now at the touch of his lips, no sparks flew, nor did she hear bells or sirens. In fact, she felt nothing.

Roger was obviously disappointed at his inability to arouse any emotion in her. Reluctantly he released her and stepped back, surveying her regretfully, the way an art dealer at an auction might study a precious painting he has just lost to another bidder.

On the drive home Julie quickly forgot about the kiss. Her thoughts were on Ned Baxter and the bold way in which he had stood up to the senator. Once again she wondered how she could have forgotten such a handsome face.

No sooner had Julie entered the office on Tuesday than the telephone rang. To her surprise Tracy Brooks was on the line, asking to meet her for brunch at the Pastry Palace. There was a note of urgency in her voice, so despite the short notice and a heavy work schedule, Julie readily agreed.

The rest of the morning she had trouble concentrating. The desperation in Tracy's voice had made her uneasy. Finally, in exasperation, she put aside the project on welfare reform that she was researching for Roger. Leaning back in her chair, she wondered what matter of earthshaking importance could have prompted so early a call.

At the appointed hour she drove around the popular restaurant several times before finding a parking spot. When she got inside, Tracy, who was sipping coffee at a corner table, waved her over. "I'm sorry I'm late, but I didn't allow enough time for Washington's perennial parking problem," Julie said breathlessly.

As the waitress approached, Tracy asked, "What would you like to order?"

"Just a French-roast coffee," Julie said as she sat down.

"Chocolate torte is the specialty of the house," Tracy said. "Sure you won't try some? That way I won't feel so guilty."

"No, thanks. As much as I'd like to indulge my sweet tooth, I'll just have to exercise some self-control."

Fidgeting with her gold necklace, Tracy eyed Julie's svelte figure enviously. She turned to the waitress and said jestingly, "All my attempts to trick her into looking like me have failed. Please bring a French-roast coffee for her and a chocolate torte for me."

When the waitress had left with their order, Tracy's round face took on a more serious expression. "Thanks for coming on such short notice. I thought it would be better if we met outside your office."

"Tell me what's on your mind," Julie said, leaning forward.

The answer came quickly: "Roger."

"Oh?" Julie swallowed hard and settled back in her seat.

"I'm upset over this reference to him in the *Banner.*" Tracy reached into her pocketbook and pulled out a newspaper clipping, which she pushed across the table. Julie's eyes widened in astonishment at reading the words Tracy had underlined in red:

Last evening, before a meeting of defense contractors, Senator Roger Whitman, one of Washington's most eligible bachelors, gave a rousing speech on his favorite topic, national defense. But what about his own defenses? A gorgeous blonde with bedroom eyes and an hourglass figure appears to have captured his heart.

Julie's face turned red with anger and embarrassment.

"Roger said he was taking an aide along to that meeting. There's only one woman on his staff that attractive"—Tracy gave her an envious glance—"you."

"I'm afraid you overrate me," Julie replied, trying to remain calm, "but I did attend that event."

"Are you involved with Roger?" Tracy asked.

Although Tracy had a reputation for being blunt, Julie thought she had outdone herself this time. Fortunately the waitress returned with their order, giving Julie a chance to regain her composure. "No, I'm not," she managed to reply.

Sensing Julie's discomfort, Tracy reached over to give her a reassuring pat on the arm. "I'm sorry," she said, "but I've never been known for my tact—a distinct disadvantage for the future wife of a United States senator, don't you think?"

Tracy's apology relieved the tension between them, and her tone of resignation made Julie feel sorry for her. "Since I did the research for Roger's talk, he asked me to attend the meeting," she explained. "My duties were to get a list of names of those in attendance and to critique his speech." Her voice hardened as she added, "Surely you're not going to take seriously anything that newspaper prints. Its editors and columnists have never had one good thing to say about Roger."

"Maybe I did overreact," Tracy admitted, her chubby fingers nervously drumming the tabletop, "but when I read it, I came unglued."

"I know who's responsible for writing that trash," Julie said, angrily squeezing the newspaper clipping into a ball.

"You do?" Tracy exclaimed in surprise.

"Yes." Julie swallowed her coffee in nervous gulps, as if trying to extinguish the rage burning within her. "A reporter by the name of Ned Baxter. He was also at the meeting. Although he made it obvious he was no admirer of Roger, I never thought he'd resort to writing such garbage." She threw the crumpled clipping down on the table to emphasize her disgust.

Tracy stared at her so forlornly that Julie's

heart twisted. "I believe you," Tracy said, "but I still feel that Roger's interested in you."

"Don't be silly," Julie said. "I'm just another staffer to him."

"Unfortunately my female intuition tells me otherwise. But I can't blame him," Tracy said with a sigh. "You're a very attractive woman." It was as if Tracy, despite all her expensive finery—a silk dress and an array of gold jewelry—now realized the futility of trying to compete with the elegance of the young blonde sitting across from her in a simple beige cotton skirt and white jersey.

"I think of Roger as my employer—nothing more," Julie assured Tracy.

"I know you have scruples," Tracy replied. "That's more than I can say for too many others in this town."

Never before had Julie heard the gentle, fun-loving woman speak with such bitterness.

"If you did find him desirable, you'd have every right to pursue him," Tracy continued as she took a forkful of her torte. "It's not as if Roger and I were married."

Tracy's words conveyed her underlying resignation, and again Julie felt a pang of sympathy for her. "I'm not in the habit of stealing what belongs to someone else," Julie said gently.

Tracy looked at her for a long time before saying, "I suppose you're wondering why I'd want to marry him when I have such doubts and suspicions."

"The thought did cross my mind," Julie confessed. Summoning her courage, she added, "Marriage has to be built on trust, something the two of you don't seem to have."

The tears welling in Tracy's eyes ended Julie's brief lecture. "I'm hopelessly in love with him," Tracy sobbed, reaching into her purse for a tissue, "but I know he doesn't feel the same way about me."

"Love shouldn't be a one-way street," Julie said. "Stand up to Roger."

"That's easier said than done. Reason tells me to forget him, but my heart won't listen," she said, struggling to control her tears. "Sometimes I wish my father had never gotten involved with launching Roger's campaign for the Senate. If it weren't for Dad's money and influence, I know Roger would never have given me a second look."

"Don't talk like that," Julie chided gently.

"Oh, it's true," she said, dabbing at her reddened eyes. "We're always told that beauty is only skin-deep. I naively thought that Roger might begin to see that deep down inside I have some desirable personal qualities."

"You certainly do," Julie said enthusiastically. "You have kindness, generosity, a sense of humor, and openness—just to name a few of them."

"I'm afraid you flatter me."

"No, it's the truth," Julie told her, unwilling to see the other go on torturing herself.

"But Roger doesn't care about personal qualities," Tracy said. "All he wants is a beautiful woman he can show off to others. I'm not that woman."

Julie blushed at Tracy's underlying meaning.

"As an incumbent senator he no longer has to rely on my family contacts, my company campaign contributions, or me." Tracy's voice trailed off to a whisper as she said, "Still I'd give up everything I have for him."

Julie felt compelled to break the awkward silence that followed. "Roger is lucky to have you."

"I wish he thought so." Then Tracy tried for a smile and said, "Thanks for listening to me. If you ever decide to get out of this messy political business, you can always make a good living as a counselor."

Tracy insisted on paying for the brunch, and together they walked out the door. Outside on the bustling sidewalk, she shook Julie's hand warmly, saying, "I want to thank you again for putting up with me in there."

"That's why I was born with such large ears," Julie replied good-naturedly.

"You mean you actually have a flaw?"

"If you look closely, you'll find a lot of them," Julie said lightly.

"I doubt it," Tracy said, unable to conceal her envy of Julie's blond beauty. As Julie was searching for more words of encouragement, Tracy asked, "What on earth brought you to Washington?"

For an instant Julie hesitated, fearing that Tracy might still consider her a serious rival for Roger's affections. With complete candor, she replied, "I had just received my degree in government, and I wanted to find out firsthand how the democratic process works. Being an idealist I also thought I might be able to contribute something to my country. Roger was visiting my father, and when he suggested I come to work for him in the nation's capital, I jumped at the chance." With a pensive smile, she continued, "I also needed to put a little more distance between my doting father and me."

Not sounding at all jealous, Tracy said, "Your sincerity and compassion are refreshing. Don't ever let the wheelers and dealers of this city change you."

With that compliment she turned and walked away. Filled with a strange sense of foreboding, Julie watched her go.

On the drive back to the office Julie tried to keep her thoughts from running wild. She had been shocked by the drastic personality change in the once happy, carefree Tracy, whom she had come to know so well from stints of volunteer work at Roger's office.

Then Julie considered the lack of communication between Tracy and Roger. While he made light of their relationship and had implied to Julie that they had come to a mutual parting of the ways, Tracy had confessed to being hopelessly in love with him. How could they be poles apart on such an important issue as their love for each other? The only logical answer was that Roger was getting ready to cast Tracy aside.

A pang of guilt stabbed at Julie as she thought about his kiss, which, of course, she had not mentioned to Tracy. After all, he was the one who had initiated the kiss, and she certainly hadn't responded to it. Even now she was puzzled by her low-key reaction. Despite being somewhat attracted to him, she had felt nothing.

Lately she had made a point of discouraging his interest in her. But the more she did so, the greater his romantic zeal became. If he were to break up with Tracy—and Julie fervently hoped he wouldn't do such a thing—she knew he wouldn't have any trouble finding another woman to take Tracy's place. In Washington, a politically powerful bachelor was always in great demand. She had to admit that when dressed in one of his impressive, three-piece suits, he looked very distinguished—even if it was in a stiff, self-centered way.

But why was he pursuing Julie so relentlessly? Was he so used to getting everything he wanted that whatever was denied him—in this case Julie herself—became all the more desirable? Or did he, as Tracy had hinted, want Julie just so he could show her off to others? Julie knew only one thing for certain: She liked and respected Tracy too much to come between her and the man she loved so deeply.

Her feelings toward Ned Baxter alternated between anger and disappointment. Despite their earlier exchanges of harsh words, there had been something about the dark, ruggedly built young man that appealed to her.

Grudgingly she had to admit she had overreacted when their boats collided. She realized that she would have behaved with even less civility if he had slammed into her. Frustration had made her quickly dismiss his good qualities, such as calmness and sound judgement during a crisis. After all, hadn't he promptly uprighted her sailboat and maneuvered his own waterlogged skiff around so that the tide had carried it to the island? Once there, hadn't he rowed out and retrieved her drifting sailboat?

During their second encounter she had been impressed with the confident way in which he had stood up to Roger. Not only did he hold his own but he soon had Roger on the defensive. She had never seen anyone manage that before.

Then Julie remembered the newspaper item Tracy had shown her, and once more she was furious at Ned. How could she ever have thought he had integrity? Now she scoffed at her own naivete. Didn't his "Washington Whispers" column in the *Banner* prove she was really a poor judge of character?

Chapter Three

Among Roger's office staff Julie had soon distinguished herself as an excellent researcher. Since so much of the senator's time was spent on political issues and pending legislation, her talent was in great demand. Increasingly she found herself in the congressional library working on various projects.

A few days after her meeting with Tracy she was there, in the stacks, doing background research on a Supreme Court nominee whose candidacy Roger opposed. She was leaning over in search of a certain call number. "Just my luck," she murmured in frustration, realizing the desired book was missing from its proper place on the shelf. As she straightened up, she inadvertently bumped into the person next to her, sending his armful of books crashing to the floor. Turning to apologize, she was shocked to find herself face-to-face with Ned

Baxter. "Oh, not you again!" she blurted out disdainfully.

"I'm beginning to think you really dislike me," he said.

"That's putting it mildly."

He shook his head. "Maybe you'll surprise me someday by acting civil."

"You don't know the meaning of the word."

He tried to end the fight by saying, "I suggest we declare a truce."

But Julie continued her unrelenting attack. "After what you've done? Don't make me laugh."

"What are you talking about?" For the first time anger flashed in his eyes.

"You do write the 'Washington Whispers' column, don't you?" she demanded accusingly.

He winced at the sarcasm in her voice. "Frankly, I no longer—"

In her haste to lash out, she interrupted him. "You obviously get your kicks hurting people. I want you to know that this time you've succeeded with that nonsense in last week's *Banner* linking Roger and me romantically. I've begun to wonder what rock you crawled out from under."

When she ran out of words to hurl at him, she gave him a withering look and tried to walk by him, but he blocked her way. His sudden move caught her by surprise.

"Oh, no, you don't!" he exclaimed before she

could protest. "I refuse to let you go sailing off into the sunset. This time you're going to remain and hear my side of the story."

She bit her lip at this reference to her sudden flight from the island after the boat mishap. For an instant she thought about forcing her way past him but the smoldering look in his dark eyes made her dismiss that idea.

"As I was saying before I was so rudely interrupted," he said, "I no longer work for the *Banner.* Besides, I know there couldn't possibly be a romance between you and Whitman. He's incapable of loving anybody but himself."

"Then why were you spying on him at the annual meeting of defense contractors?"

He laughed. "I assure you I can think of more interesting things to do than spy on the likes of him. I was there to gather some material for a book I'm writing."

"What's the title?" she asked sarcastically. "*How to Destroy a United States Senator in One Easy Lesson?*"

"For your information the title happens to be *Washington Payola,*" he retorted.

"Just what do you and that poor excuse for a newspaper have against Roger?" she demanded, irked by his condescending manner.

"I can speak only for myself," he replied, shaking his head to emphasize his strong dislike for the man. "I consider him a pompous airhead whose sole contribution to the Senate has been to corner the market on patriotism by wrapping himself in the American flag."

"Are you finished with your speech?" she demanded.

"Yes, I think we've both exhausted the boring subject of Roger Whitman." Although he still barred her way, his tone was conciliatory. "Let me assure you again that I didn't write that column. There were several reporters from the *Banner* in the lounge that evening. I can only assume it was written by one of them." Noting her look of skepticism, he added, "If you'll telephone the editor, I'm sure he'll confirm what I've just told you."

All during their argument he had looked her in the eye and shown remarkable self-control. The sincerity and frankness of his explanation had disarmed her, and as much as she tried to resist, she found herself believing him. She frowned petulantly, unwilling to give in to his persuasive powers.

He found her displeasure amusing.

When she could no longer tolerate his smiling scrutiny, she asked indignantly, "Is something the matter?"

"Has anyone ever told you that you're beautiful when you're angry?"

That, of course, just made her angrier.

Posing thoughtfully with his free hand under his chin, he said, "Then again, I've never seen you any other way, have I?"

Before she could think of a comeback to that, a security guard peered at them from around the corner of the stacks and asked her, "Are you okay?"

"Yes," she said.

"Then why are you arguing so loudly with him?" He cast a wary eye at Ned.

"It's just a lovers' quarrel," Ned chimed in, seizing the opportunity to slip an arm around her waist.

Julie was so surprised that words failed her.

"May I remind you that this is the congressional library, not a marriage-counseling center," the officer told her, raising a shaggy eyebrow questioningly.

Embarrassed, she blurted out, "We're not married."

"Not yet," Ned said, tightening his grip, "but I'm doing my best to convince her."

As she looked up at him to refute his words, his lips pressed down upon hers. Caught off guard, she could offer only token resistance. As he drew her even more securely within the circle of his arms, the scent of his after-shave lotion overpowered her.

His kiss was exciting—so much so she could feel her heart leaping and her knees quivering. She had no idea how long it lasted, but she could have sworn she heard bells and fireworks somewhere in the distance.

The guard's presence forced her to fight for

control. Regaining her composure, she tore herself from Ned's embrace and put a more respectable distance between them. Strangely enough, her reaction was one of embarrassment, not outrage at the liberty he had just taken.

With a perceptive smile, the guard turned to Ned. "Young man," he said, "I was just about to escort you out of here. That just goes to show what a poor judge of character I am."

Ned smiled innocently.

Shifting his attention to Julie, the guard said, "If I were you, miss, I'd marry him and get it over with."

"I—I'm afraid you've got this all wrong," she stammered.

"There's an old Chinese saying that a picture is worth a thousand words," he replied, lifting the visor of his cap to scratch his head. "Believe me, I just saw a portrait of true love."

All the while, Ned stood there with an amused expression, nodding in agreement to everything the man said.

"I wish you both well," the guard continued, "but in the future please do your courting in a more suitable place." Pointing to the fallen books, he added, "And please pick those up before you leave." Then he turned and walked away.

A few minutes before, Julie had vented all her pent-up fury on Ned over an insulting article she thought he had written. Now, after hc had stolen a kiss from her, she harbored no ill will toward him. She couldn't understand it. Alone with him she was beginning to feel a certain vulnerability. "You shouldn't have done that," she managed to say, her voice lacking any real conviction.

"I've been wanting to do that ever since I first met you out on the bay." He loomed over her with an easy smile.

"You certainly could have fooled me," she retorted, alluding to his rude behavior toward her in the chilly waters of Paradise Cove.

"I admit I lost my temper back then," he said.

"That's putting it mildly." She was still reeling from the potent effects of his kiss.

"I hardly need a lesson in self-control from someone who has a temper tantrum if I so much as look at her," he said. "I was hoping you'd understand and forgive my reaction—after all, it isn't every day I get rammed by a sailboat—but I can see you're too stubborn."

"At least I'm consistent—that's more than I can say for you!" Stung by his criticism, she snapped her words.

"Oh, yes, that you are," he replied roguishly. "But I'm no longer complaining about your poor navigational skills. If it weren't for that collision, you and I might never have met."

"For me that would have been a blessing."

Once again he flashed his devastating smile.

"Am I free to go now or must I shout for the security guard?" She was struggling desperately to shake off the aftereffects of his kiss.

With a mock bow he gallantly stepped aside to allow her to pass. For some reason she found herself reluctant to move past him, and instead stooped down to gather up the books.

"You don't have to do that," he said, leaning over to take them from her hand.

Her feelings toward him were becoming confused. "Since I was responsible for knocking them to the floor, the least I can do is pick them up," she replied matter-of-factly.

As his eyes caught and held hers, he asked, "Are you sure you won't consider calling a truce between us?"

"I'm afraid that won't be necessary," she said as they both straightened up. "I've said all I want to say to you. I have no intention of running into you again."

"I wouldn't be so sure of that." He spoke in a casual, jesting way. "I'm beginning to think the fates may be trying to tell us something."

"I'm a realist, not a fatalist." She tossed her hair across her shoulders in a gesture of defiance.

As she brushed past him, he said, almost as an afterthought, "Oh, Julie."

She stopped abruptly and turned to face him

again, inwardly pleased to havc an excuse not to leave. "Yes?"

"I bet you're even more beautiful when you smile."

Suddenly she felt too susceptible to his charm. "Isn't it a shame you'll never find out!" she retorted. Then she whirled around and strode out of the room, her footsteps echoing on the marble floor.

Going down the steps of the library to the sidewalk below, she looked up and saw the sun peeking through the overcast sky. A pensive smile curved the corners of her mouth. It was going to be a good day after all, she thought.

Chapter Four

"Good morning, Julie!" The cursory greeting came from Roger. He was rushing to check his schedule, which Mrs. Canterbury, his secretary, maintained with scrupulous care. Before Julie could respond, he had disappeared around a corner, leaving her smiling in amusement. His hectic pace often drew that kind of reaction from her. If he wasn't shuffling the movers and shakers of America in and out of his office, he was racing around the capital to a roll-call vote in the Senate chamber, a briefing at the State Department, or a photograph session with the President. Although she was aware of the great demands upon his time, she felt no sympathy, for she knew how much he enjoyed the pomp and pageantry of his office.

A thin, silver-haired woman, his secretary had the efficiency of a robot and the patience of a saint. She zealously protected Roger from the intrusions of the outside world and, at the of each working day, went over his ˊith him.

h Julie worked primarily as a re- ıe also was assigned to handle some ....tor's most difficult and demanding constituencies. Among them was the Wilderness Coalition. Their leader, Paul Sarkis, had called her several times that week, demanding to know what the senator's position was on the ozone problem.

So yesterday she had gone to Mrs. Canterbury to get an appointment with Roger to discuss that issue. She had squeezed Julie into his tight schedule this morning right after his first appointment with the president of a credit-card association. Julie knew that that businessman was coming to ask Roger to oppose any legislation that put a limit on the interest charged to credit-card holders.

When she arrived at Roger's office, he was still in conference. Ten minutes later his door swung open and he came out, dutifully escorting the visitor to the outer door. "Thanks for your cooperation on this crucial matter," the businessman said enthusiastically. "You can count on the full support of me and my colleagues in your upcoming reelection bid." With that remark, he grasped the senator's hand so eagerly that Julie thought he might try to kiss it.

As the door closed behind him, she shook

her head sadly. *So much for protecting the interests of the American consumer,* she thought. Recently she had become disillusioned with Roger's lukewarm stands on a host of important national issues. To her dismay, he even had acquiesced to sharp budget cuts in Social Security benefits and the student-loan program—two appropriations he had championed vigorously during his election campaign. What annoyed her even more was the cavalier way in which he so blithely dismissed any questions about his resolve on these issues. His favorite response was "He who fights and runs away lives to fight another day." Lately he was doing a lot more running than fighting.

"The senator will see you now." The voice of Mrs. Canterbury jarred her out of her musing.

Whenever Julie entered Roger's office, she felt as if she were in a museum. His long, highly polished mahogany desk, neatly set with a telephone, desk blotter, and expensive writing utensils, served more for show than work. The oriental rug, the Ming vase, and the portrait of Roger's hero, Daniel Webster, glowering down at her added to her feeling of uneasiness. She swallowed hard and went inside.

Motioning her to a wooden armchair next to his desk, he closed the door and sat down in a high-backed swivel chair. He reminded her of a king sitting on a throne and ready to send decrees to all parts of his realm.

"I just need a moment of your time to talk about the Wilderness Coalition," she said apologetically.

With a grimace at her mention of that organization, he replied, "I suppose Paul Sarkis and his merry band of nature lovers want to know what I'm doing about acid rain."

"Not exactly," she replied, opening her notebook. "This time they're asking about your position on the ozone problem."

"Hmm," he said, leaning back in his chair, momentarily lost in deep thought. "Why can't we just tell him there's a congressional committee studying it?" he burst out.

"Because that's what we told him about the acid-rain issue."

"Oh, really?" he replied, nonplussed. After a lengthy pause, he asked, "Haven't they requested me to speak before their group next month?"

"Yes, on the twenty-fifth."

"Since I want their support in my bid for re-election, you'd better tell them I'll be there on that date to speak about the threat of pollution to the ozone layer," he said, swinging around in his chair. "Just make sure I get some answers to the problem by then."

"Fine," she said, closing her notebook and rising.

"Don't leave," he said, gesturing for her to remain seated. "I have something else I'd like to discuss with you."

"Oh?" she replied, once again sitting down.

"Tracy insisted on meeting me at the airport last night. She was very upset about that article in the *Banner.*"

Julie had noticed recently that he was trying hard to put as much distance as possible between himself and Tracy. "I can understand that," she said coolly. "I wasn't exactly thrilled about it myself."

Her lack of emotion at being linked romantically with him in the newspaper column seemed to surprise him. "Naturally I just assumed it was the work of Baxter," he said. "But when I called the editor to complain, guess what?"

"He wasn't the culprit," she said with feigned nonchalance.

"That's right." He looked at her curiously. "How'd you know that?"

"While doing research at the congressional library, I ran into Ned and—"

"Ned?" he interrupted, raising an eyebrow in obvious displeasure at her use of his first name. "I do hope you're not getting too familiar with him."

"I don't think you have to worry about that," she replied, her tone hardly offering the reassurance he sought. "He kept insisting that he was no longer working for the newspaper."

"Much as I'd enjoy pointing the finger of suspicion at him, I'm afraid I can't." His face mirrored his disappointment. "I was told he resigned from the staff last month." Unable to resist poking fun at Ned, he said, "Isn't the editor a lucky fellow?" When his attempt at humor failed to bring a smile to her face, he asked, "What's troubling you?"

"Unfortunately I gave him a piece of my mind." Her voice was tinged with regret.

"I'm sure that must have raised his intelligence quotient by a hundred points."

His second effort at ridiculing Ned also failed to make her smile. She just sighed and said, "I really made a fool of myself with wild accusations."

"I wouldn't lose any sleep over it." Looking at her suspiciously, he probed, "I do hope you're not interested in him."

"No, not really," she said untruthfully, her fingers toying with the cover of the notebook lying on her lap.

"I'm reluctant to share you with anyone else—least of all with Baxter," he whispered, his hand sliding across the desktop to take hold of hers.

Usually Roger was all business in the office, going out of his way to avoid even the slightest hint of impropriety. Now he had violated his own cardinal rule, and Julie was totally unprepared to deal with his romantic gesture. "Please, Roger," she blurted out, pulling her hand away.

"What's wrong with you?" he asked, his eyes blazing at her accusingly. "Lately you've been as cold to me as an Arctic blast. It's Tracy, isn't it?"

"Yes," she confessed, avoiding his gaze.

"I've told you that it's all over between us. After my reelection campaign, I'll make a clean break with her, I swear." He raised his right hand as if taking an oath. "Since a lot of money comes to my campaign from her company, right now I'd prefer not to rock the boat. Surely you can understand that?"

"Yes, of course. I believe that's what they call political expediency." Her words were spoken with cool precision.

Irritated, he said, "Politics is considered the art of compromise, and I admit to having done my share."

"For Tracy, love's not a political game," she shot back.

"Whose side are you on?" he asked, obviously annoyed.

"No one's," she said with a heavy sigh, "but I have to do what's right."

The corners of his mouth curled in impatience. "Do us both a favor and stop being so noble. It's about time you realized life is one big political game. How do you think I got where I am today?"

"I sometimes wonder."

His gaze swept over her once again as he said, "For the daughter of Simon Hartwell, you sometimes surprise me."

"What's that supposed to mean?"

"Just that your father plays the political game better than most." He leaned back on his chair with a smirk.

"I wouldn't know about that."

"Well, I do," he retorted. "You don't think those government contracts his company gets come from the tooth fairy, do you?"

The force of his reply caught her off guard. "Frankly, I've never paid much attention to his business matters," she said.

"Thanks to me, his company made over twelve million dollars in profit last year." His voice was full of the arrogance she had come to loathe.

"And just what did you get for all your generous support?" she asked.

"A guarantee of both the company's and your father's complete moral and financial support for my reelection campaign."

"Is that all?"

"Of course there are certain other favors I demand," he said, his eyes raking over her.

She was tempted to remind him that she wasn't one of them, but held her tongue.

He leaned forward on his chair and studied her with a searching gravity. "Do you know that your father may become the next president of Acme Electronics?"

How could I forget? she thought. With the death of his wife and Julie's long absences at college and work, his job had become his whole life. Now his last important career objective was to serve as president of Acme Electronics. It had become his obsession. She shuddered to think what might happen if he failed to achieve it. "So I've heard," she replied, trying to sound casual.

"As the comptroller, he's worked closely with me on many projects." His voice had a patronizing quality that grated on her. "I've gotten to know him well—almost as well as you."

She squirmed in her seat. He was sending her hidden messages that she was reluctant to decode.

"He's a good man," he acknowledged.

She wanted to say that it was too bad her father didn't feel the same way about him. Instead she replied, "I couldn't agree with you more, but then I'm prejudiced on that subject."

"Fortunately I'm in a unique position to help him get what he wants," Roger said with an insinuating smile.

"Yes, I'm sure you are," she murmured uneasily.

"But I wouldn't think of using my influence on his behalf." After a pregnant pause, he added, "Unless, of course, *you* asked me."

Suddenly she felt as if she were sitting next to a villain out of some melodrama. Anger welled up within her. Roger was playing a dangerous game with her, and she didn't like it. He wanted her to beg him to help her father get the promotion. She knew such a gesture would cost her dearly. As much as she wanted to help her father, she had no intention of submitting to blackmail.

The ringing of Roger's telephone came as a welcome relief. When he got tied up in a conversation about one of his nominees to the Naval Academy, Julie seized the opportunity to steal out of his office.

For several days afterward Julie fumed. She had seen another side of Roger, one that she detested. He knew how much her father's promotion meant to her and had promptly tried to exploit it. In a crafty, suggestive way he had made his offer to use his influence on her father's behalf dependent upon her willingness to respond favorably to his romantic advances. Even now as she thought about his ploy, she could feel herself getting furious. Of course, her answer would always be a resounding no.

When she had calmed down, she decided her only reasonable course of action was to put more distance between them. But it wasn't easy. Roger acted as if nothing had happened.

If anything, he became more ardent in his pursuit of her.

A few weeks later he even chose her to receive his Happy Warrior Award. The trophy of a smiling face, along with a check for five hundred dollars—both designed to improve staff morale—went to the member of his staff whom he felt had made the greatest contribution that year to the success of his political organization. At the formal luncheon she felt awkward standing on the dais to receive her prize, and she cringed as he raised a wineglass with a flourish and shouted, "A toast to Julie Hartwell, without whose tireless efforts I could never have been transformed from a mere politician into a serious statesman." With a devilish wink in her direction he added, "Who knows where she'll take me in the future?"

"All the way to the White House," some of the more vocal—or slightly tipsy—members of his staff shouted.

Julie was beginning to have second thoughts about continuing to work for the senator. Whenever he was in his office, he openly displayed his interest in her. To avoid him she made a conscious effort to spend a good part of those days away on some errand or project.

For that reason, one morning not long afterward, she was once again in the Library of

Congress doing some research on poverty in America. Roger needed the information for use in a seminar he was scheduled to chair at a convention of social-service providers. Because she was having trouble concentrating, only by exerting extreme willpower was she able to finish the task. Although the sheer beauty of the interior of the library could be distracting, today it wasn't the Corinthian columns, marble stairways, or vaulted ceilings that caused her mind to wander. Ned Baxter was the culprit. She hadn't seen him for several months, and now he suddenly dominated her thoughts. As she wandered aimlessly throughout the ornate building, she was hoping she might find him leaning against one of the stacks or sitting at a corner carrel. She even climbed to the gallery and surveyed the octagonal reading room below. Oblivious to the statues, carvings, and stained-glass windows, she hungered for a glimpse of Ned. But her search was in vain.

Once outside she walked back toward her office. The sight of the Capitol on her left and the Supreme Court Building on her right—imposing symbols of national power—humbled her. The last time she had felt that way was upon her arrival in Washington. Then she had devoted all her spare time to visiting major attractions like the Lincoln Memorial and the Washington Monument. She had toured the White House, watched a film at the

National Air and Space Museum, walked the corridors of the National Portrait Gallery, and attended a concert at the John F. Kennedy Center for the Performing Arts. In her initial enthusiasm, she had acted just like one of the fifteen million tourists who descend upon the capital each year.

The longer she remained, the more jaded she became. And she didn't like that feeling. She realized that with its museums, monuments, parks, and elaborate architecture, the city was a worthy showpiece for such a strong and powerful nation. Still, if she had to choose between living in Washington or Paradise Cove, there was no doubt in her mind what her choice would be.

When she arrived back at the office, she went directly to the conference room to put the information she had gathered into chart form for Roger's use at his upcoming seminar. No sooner had she settled down behind the long table covered with white cardboard than she heard the familiar voice of Tracy Brooks. "Is Roger in?" she demanded.

From her tone, Julie was thankful to be hidden from view.

"Yes, but right now he's meeting with an ambassador," Mrs. Canterbury replied with her usual aplomb. "After that he's off to the Defense Department for a briefing."

"Frankly, I don't care if he's scheduled to

meet with an emissary from the Martians," Tracy said in a voice that left no doubt about her resolve. "I intend to see him before he leaves the building."

"Is he expecting you?" Mrs. Canterbury asked graciously.

"You must be kidding," Tracy said. "He won't even talk to me on the telephone."

"I can't say how long he'll be in there," Mrs. Canterbury said, trying tactfully to discourage Tracy from staying.

The strategem didn't work. "That's no problem," Tracy replied with a wistful sadness. "Lately I have nothing but time."

For the next twenty minutes the nervous staccatolike tapping of Tracy's shoe on the tiled floor prevented Julie from concentrating on her work. Finally Roger's door squeaked open. He and the ambassador walked to the outer office, where they exchanged parting pleasantries.

After the other man left, Roger turned his attention to his unexpected visitor. "Oh, Tracy, it's you." His voice was noticeably lacking in enthusiasm. Since he couldn't avoid her without creating a nasty scene, Julie knew he'd have to invite her into his office. His invitation wasn't long in coming. "Let's go inside where we can talk," he said stiffly.

As he closed the office door after her, a cushion of air popped open the door leading to the conference room where Julie was working. She didn't want to eavesdrop, but she knew it would embarrass them if she made her presence known by getting up to close the door.

"What can I do for you?" she heard Roger ask Tracy officiously.

Tracy sounded exasperated. "I'm not one of your constituents, and I resent your talking down to me. In case you've forgotten, I used to be your fiancée."

Her use of the past tense startled Julie.

"I'm fully aware of who you are," he retorted.

"Then why can't I even get an appointment to see you?"

"Stop exaggerating," he said impatiently. "You know how busy I am."

"Too busy to return any of my telephone calls," she said accusingly. When he chose not to answer, she added, "I'd have a lot more respect for you if you'd stop playing games and tell me to my face that you no longer want anything to do with me."

"All right, then," he said coldly. "I no longer want anything to do with you. If I've been less than candid recently, it's only because I didn't want to hurt you."

"Hurt me?" she replied with a scornful laugh. "For me you've become a master in the art of torment."

"Let's do without the histrionics," he said.

"You wanted the truth and I'm giving it to you."

"It's Julie Hartwell, isn't it?"

"Julie has nothing to do with my decision," Roger said.

"Good! Because she's much too good for you." Suddenly, Tracy's voice softened. "Oh, Roger! What's gone wrong between us?" she asked.

He laughed cruelly. "Why don't you take a look in the mirror?"

"I can't help what I am," she sobbed.

"That's precisely the problem," he said. "My political future is unlimited, and I want a wife who has poise, dignity, and beauty—not a woman who belongs on a fat farm."

Julie wanted to run from the room, but she sat frozen in shock at what she was hearing on the other side of the wall.

"You're despicable!" Tracy cried. "You use people and then discard them like empty milk cartons. I'm not going to let you do that to me."

"I'm afraid you have no choice in the matter," Roger said. "Now, if you'll excuse me, I have to leave for a meeting." Julie heard him walk to the door, then pause. "And I don't want you showing up here again, understand?"

"And to think I once loved you!" Tracy said.

"You'll get over it. You may even be lucky enough to find another man to take my place.

It's amazing what money will do—even for someone like you."

With that verbal jab, Roger opened the door and left. He stopped at Mrs. Canterbury's desk just long enough to say, "Be sure to see that Miss Brooks gets safely out of the building, will you?"

No sooner had the outer door closed behind him, than the sound of breaking pottery came from his office. Instinctively, Julie jumped to her feet. She almost dashed into his office, but she realized her presence would only embarrass Tracy.

Meanwhile, Mrs. Canterbury had already entered, and she exclaimed, "Good heavens, Miss Brooks! You've just smashed the senator's Ming vase to smithereens."

"Yes, so I have," Tracy replied serenely. "Tell him that it will be a lot easier to mend than my broken heart." She slammed the door behind her.

Chapter Five

When Julie arrived at the office the following Monday morning, she didn't know that she was in for one of the most difficult weeks of her life. At nine-thirty the entire staff was hastily called to a meeting in the conference room. Since Roger was supposed to be at a budget meeting, she was surprised when he appeared, ashen faced and shaken. "Today I have some tragic news to report," he said, steadying himself against the edge of the table. "Tracy Brooks died last night." Everyone gasped, and Roger paused before he added, "Her death has been ruled a suicide. I don't have to tell you what the loss of that vibrant and enthusiastic woman means to me personally—"

Julie felt momentarily faint, and the hypocrisy in Roger's words of praise sickened her.

Attending the wake the next day also caused her great distress. For several hours she sat in the ornate funeral parlor, staring across at the casket surrounded by floral wreaths. Meanwhile Roger was moving among the clusters of friends and relatives, offering comfort. So convincing was his performance that had she not heard with her own ears just how shabbily he had treated Tracy a few days earlier, she would have believed his sorrow was genuine.

On the day of the funeral Julie was among the throng of people gathered at the church to pay their final respects to the woman with the laughing eyes and ready smile. With her Porsche she joined the cortege wending its way slowly past Tracy's favorite places—the stately Colonial row home on the quiet, tree-lined street in Georgetown, the country club, and suburban headquarters of Brooks Securities. At the cemetery, Julie had just dropped a red rose into the open grave and turned to walk back to her car when she felt a hand firmly on her arm. "Keep moving," Roger commanded. "I've told her relatives I'm driving back with you."

Still miffed at his coarse treatment of Tracy, Julie was too upset to protest his company.

Once safely inside her Porsche, he exclaimed, "Whew! Am I glad that ordeal's over."

She glared at him as she turned on the ignition.

"What's wrong with you?" he demanded.

"Right now they're throwing dirt over the

body of a wonderful woman who died needlessly, and you have the insensitivity to ask me what's wrong." The car was moving through the black wrought-iron gate.

"Go ahead and take your anger out on me if it makes you feel better," he retorted.

"I can't help it if I feel some guilt," she said icily.

"You're blaming yourself needlessly," he said. "Tracy's been under the care of a psychiatrist for a long time."

"I don't believe it," Julie exclaimed, stopping for a red light and staring across at him.

"It's the truth," he insisted. "She put on a good front, but under that veneer of good humor and spontaneity lay a frightened and insecure woman."

"But why?" She lifted a hand from the steering wheel to emphasize her bewilderment.

"Let's face it, she had no confidence in herself," he said. "She didn't feel she deserved to be wealthy, she wasn't happy with her looks, and she didn't think she was intelligent enough to run the family business. Need I say more?"

"You should have handled her more carefully."

Her reproach drew a swift response from him. "What are you talking about?"

"When Tracy came storming into your office last week, I heard everything the two of you said," she blurted out.

The color drained from his face. "Since when have you started eavesdropping on me?" he asked.

"I was in the conference room, working on your charts," she replied, finding herself on the defensive. "The door leading to your office was slightly ajar."

"Then you heard her say she wanted the truth," he said defensively, trying to justify his actions on that day. "That's exactly what I gave her."

"You weren't being truthful, you were being cruel."

"Do you know how long I avoided discussing the subject of breaking up with her?" he asked. "I couldn't let it go on forever."

She shook her head, muttering, "Somehow you always make everything sound so easy."

"Believe me, it wasn't easy—not with Tracy." His response held a note of impatience. "She was a very jealous person. Naturally my job brings me into contact with all kinds of people—including attractive members of the opposite sex. She couldn't stand seeing me with another woman. At such times, no matter what the circumstances were, she would fly into a rage."

When the corners of Julie's mouth twisted into an expression of doubt, he argued his case more forcefully. "Surely you recall how upset she got over that article in the *Banner?*"

Julie nodded, for she would never forget it. Despite his vigorous defense of his actions, she remained skeptical about his true motives. She felt that deep down inside he was gloating that Tracy was out of the way.

"On the other hand, *you* could hardly care less about any other woman in my life," he said, intruding upon her thoughts, "but I intend to change all that. Sometimes even sorrowful events have a way of working out for the best."

Upset at the impropriety of his last remark, she turned the steering wheel so sharply to go down a side street that the force hurled him against the passenger door. Soon his office building loomed up ahead, and she was relieved to pull to an abrupt halt by the front entrance. Turning to him, she blurted out, "I'm resigning from your staff effective immediately."

"I refuse to hear of it," he replied, dismissing her announcement with a wave of his hand. "You're taking this whole matter too personally. I want you to go home and relax. After a good night's sleep, you'll see things differently."

She thought he'd never get out of the car, but finally he reached for the handle and opened the door. Once outside, he leaned through the open window, saying, "Besides, I couldn't survive without you." She avoided his eager eyes. "I'm flying out to California tonight for that convention," he went on. "I won't be back until the middle of next week. When I see you again, I hope you'll be in a more positive mood. After all, I didn't give you the Happy Warrior Award for nothing." With a smirk he turned and walked toward his office as she put the car in gear and pulled away.

That night she tossed and turned on her bed. The thought of Tracy's suicide made sleeping impossible, since pangs of guilt stabbed at her. With a heavy sigh she sat up and leaned against the headboard, trying desperately to find answers to the questions that now were haunting her: Had Tracy been so in love with Roger that life without him had lost all meaning? Had she become so fragile that his harsh words had pushed her over the brink? Did he taunt her into committing her last, desperate act? Hadn't Julie herself listened in disbelief to all the verbal insults he so gleefully hurled at Tracy? How could he be so self-righteous about his role in the tragedy? Had Julie herself been an unwitting accomplice?

Finally she arose and slipped out onto the balcony. At such moments she considered herself fortunate to have a nice furnished apartment in one of the more scenic parts of Washington. She had sublet it from a business associate of her father's—a parting concession to his doting nature.

To her pleasant surprise the night was unusually mild. A myriad of lights glowed in the distance, and a peaceful beauty hung over the sleeping city. Soon the cherry trees along the Tidal Basin and in the Potomac parks would be bursting into spectacular bloom, she thought.

But even now she could feel Paradise Cove beckoning. There the peepers would be singing their nocturnal serenade. Like blindfolds, the boards covering the picture windows of the summer homes along the cove would come off, revealing the breathtaking view of the bay. The boats, which were sprawled out incongruously on the grounds of the yacht club during winter, would be bobbing joyfully at their moorings.

She mentally reviewed her experiences since coming to work in the nation's capital. Again she remembered the novelty of exploring the sights of the famous city, the daily routine of her work as a staff aide, Roger's growing infatuation with her, her initial positive impressions of him, the specter of Tracy hanging over them, her own ambivalence and feelings of guilt, the suicide, and Roger's apparent relief.

She broke the evening silence, murmuring, "I'm going to return to Paradise Cove! The sooner, the better."

Having made that momentous decision, she turned and went inside to her desk. She sat down and began writing a letter:

Dear Roger,

I am resigning my position as your aide, effective immediately. By the time you read this, I will have left Washington.

There are many reasons for my decision, not the least of which is that I don't enjoy living and working in a city—even one as unique and historic as the nation's capital.

I have also found myself at odds recently with your positions on several key issues, such as national health insurance and nuclear power.

And Tracy's suicide has made my resignation necessary. Although I do not hold myself responsible for her death, I am still overwhelmed with guilt. When I first came here, I cannot deny that I found you appealing. But I knew that Tracy had you first, and I refuse to come between you, even now. You yourself have said we cannot go back, only ahead.

I do want to thank you for giving me the chance to work in Washington. I only hope that during my brief stay I was able to make some modest contributions to your organization.

I wish you continued success with your political career.

Julie

She neatly folded the letter and slipped it into an envelope, which she addressed *To Roger Whitman—personal.* Then she climbed back into bed and tried once again to sleep.

Chapter Six

That Friday Julie worked feverishly at the office to finish several projects and put all her affairs in order. In the afternoon she cleaned out her desk and brought the envelope containing her letter of resignation to Mrs. Canterbury. When Julie asked her to give it to the senator, she took it reluctantly, as if sensing the message inside. Walking out of the building for the last time, Julie felt a sense of relief.

That weekend she came to appreciate just how easy it was to leave a furnished apartment. Sunday morning, with all her possessions crammed into the rear of her sports car, she blew a farewell kiss at the familiar balcony. Then she drove away without looking back. She planned to spend the night at her father's home before driving on to Paradise Cove in the morning.

Outside the city limits she frowned, unhappy with herself for not having been more forceful in her letter of resignation. She had left so many things unsaid. She hadn't even reprimanded Roger for his earlier unflattering remarks about her father. Though she reminded herself that she had written a letter of resignation, not an indictment, she kept asking herself if she had purposely toned down her anger to avoid ruining her father's chances for his big promotion. And despite the unnerving events of the past year, was she still attracted to Roger?

Hours later, as she turned in at the stone pillars bearing brass plates engraved with the Hartwell name, those questions remained unanswered. Moving up the long driveway, she grew nostalgic at the sight of the forsythia, azalea, and rhododendron bushes, their spring buds eager to burst forth and bedazzle the beholder with the vivid colors of their flowers. Her mother, blessed with a green thumb, had planted each one with care. After her death, Mr. Hartwell, who couldn't tell a daisy from a dandelion, had hired a gardener to look after them.

She parked her Porsche in front of the spacious Colonial house, glad to get out and stretch. Her father's car wasn't parked in its usual place—a sure sign he was at work. Even a Sunday couldn't interfere with his workaholic routine, she thought.

She sauntered across the lawn, already green

with new growth. From the patio in back, she admired the neatly pruned dwarf fruit trees, their limbs also swollen with buds—another tribute to her mother's botanical talents.

Although she had a set of keys, she chose to remain outside and enjoy the mild afternoon. She stretched out on a chaise longue from which she continued to admire the scenery until, weary from the long drive, she began to doze. She didn't hear her father's footsteps on the flagstone walk, stirring only when he greeted her warmly: "Julie, this is a pleasant surprise."

Mr. Hartwell had never been a demonstrative man, but the death of his wife had changed him. Now whenever Julie returned home, he would welcome her with real affection. Today was no exception as he leaned over and embraced her. Sitting down on the picnic bench next to her, he asked, "Why are all your belongings piled into the rear of your car?"

Julie smiled, knowing that his hawklike eyes seldom missed anything. "I've quit my job," she confessed.

"Oh?"

For a man who had protested so strenuously her decision to accept the job in Washington, his response was more subdued than she had expected. "You don't approve?" she asked.

"Yes, I do," he said, showing more enthusiasm.

There was a lull in the conversation as they both watched a tree squirrel dash along a limb and scramble down a thin wire from which dangled a bird feeder. When the squirrel began consuming the seed with gusto, she said, "I can see the birds have some competition for their food."

"It's just the same with human beings," her father replied in a philosophical vein. "Somebody's always trying to claim what isn't rightfully his. And, speaking of food, you must be starving. Why don't we go out to eat?"

"I'm really not hungry," she replied. "I stopped for a bite on the road."

"At least come inside and chat while I fix myself a snack," he said, moving toward the back door. "Surely you'll have a cup of coffee?"

"Yes, of course," she agreed as she followed him.

Inside the roomy kitchen he fixed a sandwich for himself and made coffee for her. "What made you decide to quit your job?" he asked, finally taking a seat opposite her.

She had been hoping for a chance to tell him about Roger's slur, and now she had the perfect opening. "I got tired of listening to Roger boast about how he had you in his back pocket," she said.

There was an awkward silence, and then he said, "Unfortunately, Acme Electronics is heavily dependent upon government contracts."

"And Roger supplies them?" she asked bluntly.

"Yes. As a member of the Armed Services Committee, he exerts a lot of influence."

"As he so eloquently puts it, he scratches your back and you scratch his."

"I guess that's one way of putting it." A shrug of resignation accompanied his admission as he sat down again.

"And what do you have to give him in return?" she asked.

"The company raised large sums of money in support of his last campaign, and I'm sure it'll do the same thing this time."

"Is that all?" she asked persistently, stirring the contents of her cup.

He avoided her gaze, sipping his coffee. "Isn't that enough? After all, not everyone gets the chance to serve as a United States senator. And you know how Roger is about pomp, pageantry, and power."

"Yes, the trappings and prestige of the office are important to him."

"Why am I getting the feeling I'm on the witness stand?" he asked.

"Because Roger implied that you and the company were providing him with perks."

"I don't know what he's talking about." His hands trembled as he lifted his cup.

"How can you work with him when it's so obvious you can't stand him?" she asked accusingly.

"Because the company pays me well to court his favor."

"It's really to ensure your promotion, isn't it?" she asked.

"I've never made a secret of its importance to me," he admitted.

"Is it worth sacrificing your integrity for?" she blurted out.

He stared at her over his bifocals. "You certainly don't mince any words," he finally managed to say. "Like your mother, you always did have a knack for getting to the essence of a problem."

Now she regretted saying anything.

"It's more than my promotion," he told her. "The jobs of thousands of others in the company are at stake. And I've always been paid well for my services."

She reddened, knowing what he was about to remind her.

"How do you think I've managed to afford all these material comforts?" With a sweeping motion of his hand, he indicated the expensive furnishings throughout the house. After a pause, he added, "My job also paid for your college education, financed your trips to Europe, and enabled you to spend all those summers at The Gull's Way."

His words—as close he ever could come to scolding her—had struck a sensitive chord, and she ceased her questioning. On those rare occasions in the past when they had argued, he had always let her win. Sometimes she wondered how such a warm, compassionate man as her father could ever have earned a reputation for being a tough business executive. "I can't complain," she said with a sigh of resignation, "especially since I'm planning to drive out to The Gull's Way tomorrow."

"That's what it's there for," he replied, sounding relieved their discussion was over.

Suddenly a pang of guilt pricked at her. "Dad, I'm sorry for jumping all over you just now," she apologized. "I had no right to do that."

"Frankness is one of your many virtues," he replied tolerantly. "Besides, you may be right in your assessment of my motives."

"I'm afraid I'm not sure of anything anymore," she said sadly.

"What's wrong?" he asked, disturbed by her sudden change of mood.

"Lately a lot's been happening."

"Would you like to talk about it?" he asked.

"Tracy Brooks committed suicide," she told him.

"Yes, I was saddened to learn of it," he replied with genuine regret. "Although I didn't know her personally, I worked with her father on Roger's first campaign for public office."

"Her death made me think seriously about my own life."

"Death has a way of doing that," he said gently.

She didn't respond, for she realized he was referring to his own anguish over the loss of his wife.

The look of sadness on his face yielded to curiosity as he said, "Rumor has it that the senator and Tracy had broken up. Was there any truth to it?"

"I'm sure Roger viewed it that way," she said, then, when she saw the way her father was looking at her, added, "There was nothing between him and me!"

"He's definitely interested in you," he replied, still skeptical. "Whenever I see him, you're all he talks about. I just hope you're not running away from him."

His doubts about her motives prompted her to say, "There are many reasons I left Washington. Once I was there it didn't take me long to find out I'm just a country girl at heart."

"I believe I tried to tell you that very same thing before you accepted the job," he reminded her.

She nodded. "But I had to learn it the hard way."

"Unfortunately I think you inherited that nasty trait from me."

Those words made her smile. "The wheeling and dealing as well as the political intrigue turned me off," she explained. "And, frankly, I missed Paradise Cove. Tracy's suicide made me decide to leave. I'm planning to stay at Paradise Cove indefinitely, if it's all right with you."

"Of course I approve," he said. "Either you really love that place, or you're eager to get away from me."

"A little of both," she said teasingly. "But, seriously, I do have a lot of thinking to do about my future plans."

"And so do I," he replied, shaking his head.

For a long time they lingered at the table, chatting amiably. Then they cleaned up the kitchen, and, tired from her long drive, Julie went to her room to rest.

As she climbed the stairs leading to her bedroom on the second floor, she felt a strange sensation of sadness. Ever since she had first gone away to college, that same feeling would grip her whenever she returned home. Perhaps it had to do with her mother's death, her preference for the summer place at Paradise Cove, or just the mysterious process of growing up.

Her room remained just as she had left it before going off to college. The walls were adorned with her high-school banner, cheerleading pom-poms, and pictures of her favorite screen star. She smiled, recalling her shock when she learned he wore a hairpiece.

Settling onto the edge of her bed, she glanced at the mirror over the bureau. Tucked into the frame were old photographs that marked the rituals of her passage through high school—National Honor Society, cheerleading squad, senior prom, graduation. . . .

Her roving eyes stopped at a picture yellowing with age—she and her mother sailing out on the waters of Paradise Cove. *Happier days,* she thought. How quickly they had vanished when her mother's life was snuffed out by a drunken driver. For a long time afterward Julie would wake up in the middle of the night, fearing that she, too, might die that same way. Her mother's death had taught her there were many things in life over which she had no control. With a heavy sigh, she lay back against the pillow and closed her eyes.

When she awoke, the sun was peeking at her from beneath the edges of the window shades. To her shock it was eight o'clock in the morning. She jumped out of bed and rushed to take a shower. By the time she arrived downstairs, her father had left for work.

With his usual concern, he had prepared a place setting for her at the table. Smiling at his thoughtfulness, she turned on the flame under the kettle and popped two slices of bread into the toaster. As she sat down, her gaze fell upon an envelope addressed to her. Opening it, she found a legal document and a letter:

Dear Julie,

Enclosed is the deed to the summer place at Paradise Cove. I've taken the liberty of having the ownership transferred over to you. I have no real use for the property, and I know how much it means to you. Besides, your mother would have wanted you to have it.

As for yesterday, I appreciated your openness with me. You owed me no apology, for you spoke the truth. Like you, I guess I, too, have a lot of thinking to do.

Love,
Dad

P.S. I promise not to intrude upon your privacy. Please give me a call if you need anything.

Chapter Seven

Ever since Julie had left to work in the nation's capital, she had felt Paradise Cove drawing her back irresistibly. How she had longed for the sight of the gingerbread cottages with their white picket fences, and the old lighthouse, standing sentrylike and staring stolidly seaward. Now she was determined to make up for lost time. She spent endless hours sauntering along her favorite stretches of sandy beach, clambering over huge sand dunes, and crossing the wooden footbridges that spanned the salt marshes. While she was enjoying the activity of the day—sailing out on the bay, fishing off Sluiceway Point, or swimming at high tide—she often would pause to wonder why she ever had been so foolish as to have strayed so far from a town so aptly named Paradise Cove.

Her routine was a simple one. Warm, sunny days were devoted to enjoying outdoor pursuits; inclement ones, to completing household chores.

One dreary, overcast morning she had driven down to Vanderhoof's hardware store in the center of the small town to buy a shade for one of her picture windows. At the rear of the shop she found the one she wanted, but it needed to be cut down to size. As she started toward the front of the shop to get Mr. Vanderhoof's help, she stopped abruptly, unable to believe her eyes. At the cash register the bent, elderly owner was chatting amiably with Ned Baxter, who had just purchased a rod holder and fishing net.

Her first impulse was to dash up to Ned and say something clever like, "Haven't I seen you someplace before—perhaps on the Wanted posters at the post office?" Still she hesitated. Despite her fond memory of his kiss, he had, after all, taken certain liberties with her. Before she could decide the right thing to do, he left the store.

"Mr. Vanderhoof," she called, "would you mind cutting this shade to fifty inches for me?"

"Of course not," he said, walking over to her.

While he was putting the shade into the cutting machine, she asked nonchalantly, "Was that Ned Baxter you were just talking to?"

"Yes, do you know him?" he replied as he made the cut.

"Sort of," she said vaguely. "We met last summer—by accident."

"A fine young man," he said enthusiastically, shutting off the machine and removing the shade. "He's vacationed here in the past and liked it so much he decided to buy the Jenkins cabin."

"Oh?" she exclaimed in surprise.

Handing the shade to her, he added, "When he's not fishing, he's writing."

"Sounds like a great life to me," she said, accompanying him to the front of the store, where she paid for her purchase.

Outside she regretted not having approached Ned. But if he was living in the town, she was certain their paths would cross again.

Just when she was beginning to forget about her life in Washington and Tracy's suicide, Roger telephoned. His call caught her by surprise. "I'm at the airport and eager to see you again," he said as if nothing had come between them. "If you'll drive over, we can go out to eat. But I'll have to be back for my eleven-thirty flight to Washington." Before she could refuse, he added, "I won't take no for an answer. I'll be waiting for you in front of the American Airlines ticket counter." Long after he had hung up, she stood holding the receiver, wondering whether to let him wait in vain. But she relented and drove out to meet him.

In the airport the last thing she wanted was a display of affection. But Roger swept her into his arms, crushing her to his chest. The warmth of his greeting left her breathless and evoked some painful memories. She firmly pushed herself away from him.

"Absence *does* make the heart grow fonder!" he exclaimed, noting with approval her beige skirt and cream blouse with matching hair ribbon. "You look stunning," he said. "But on you, rags would look elegant."

Despite the compliment, she wasn't pleased. She certainly hadn't dressed up to impress him.

Boldly he reached over and untied the ribbon, letting her tawny hair fall about her face. "At least let your hair caress your cheeks," he said. "I prefer that natural, sensuous look."

On the way to the restaurant, even in the darkness of the car, she could feel his eyes on her. Unable to stand his scrutiny any longer, she asked, "What brought you out here?"

"I was asked to give the commencement speech at the state university," he replied with his familiar air of self-importance. "Frankly, I accepted only because it gave me an excuse to see you again."

Ignoring his remark, she said, "What kind of advice did you give the graduates?"

"I urged them to set lofty goals in life and to pursue them with reckless abandon." He released the clasp on his seat belt and edged closer to her.

Neither the meaning in his words nor the romantic maneuver went unnoticed. She breathed a sigh of relief as the Oyster Inn loomed up ahead. Pulling the car to a halt in the parking lot, she wasted no time in getting out.

As the hostess led Julie across the dimly lit, oak-beamed dining room, Roger held her arm firmly, as if fearing she might flee at the first opportunity. When they were seated at an elegantly set corner table, he cast a wary glance around. Satisfied no threat to their privacy existed, he put on his best smile and turned his attention to her. "Surely you can't be serious about not seeing me again," he said.

"I've never been more serious about anything in my life," she icily replied.

"You might at least have told me to my face rather than in a letter," he said peevishly.

"Oh, Roger!" she said with a heavy sigh. "Don't make this any more difficult than it already is."

Sensing her vulnerability, he replied, "I refuse to give you up, and I'm sure you realize I usually get what I go after."

"It wasn't my intention to come between you and Tracy," she retorted, tossing her hair across her shoulders in a display of frustration.

That gesture, emphasizing the delicacy of

her fine features, made her more desirable than ever to him. "Ah, but you did," he said, smiling suggestively.

"Then I'll never forgive myself for it." Her voice was tinged with regret.

"Will you forget about her?" he demanded impatiently. "I refuse to spend the rest of my life punishing myself." His tone softened as he added, "Besides, who could blame me for falling in love with someone as beautiful as you?"

"In case you've forgotten, you were engaged to be married to her," she said.

He shrugged. "That's ancient history. I didn't stop over here from Washington to talk about Tracy."

"Just what *did* you come for?"

"For you," he answered, reaching across the table for her hand.

Exasperated, she pulled it away quickly. "You still don't understand, do you?"

"What's there to understand? I love you, and I'm sure you love me." Despite his air of confidence, his eyes studied her closely, trying to gauge her reaction. "The election's only months away. After that, we can spend a lifetime together."

Her frown was anything but reassuring. "If only I'd never gone to work in your Washington office," she said in frustration.

"What a terrible thought." Again he

reached for her hand. "There would have been a big void in my life."

When the waitress arrived to take their orders, Julie pulled her hand away from him.

Glancing at the menu, he quickly made the selections. "Tonight we're going to celebrate," he said enthusiastically. "Bring us two orders of Lobster Alexander and a bottle of Moselle wine."

"No, miss," Julie interceded. "I'd prefer the broiled scrod."

He raised an eyebrow at her refusal to accept his menu choices. After the waitress left with their orders, he said, "I thought lobster was your favorite dish."

"My tastes have changed," she replied curtly.

"It seems they've become more plebeian," he muttered before changing the subject. "I expect to be visiting Argentina as a member of the Committee on Foreign Relations," he informed her boastfully.

Two ducks floating on the placid surface of the pond below had caught her attention, and she hadn't heard a word he said. "What do you find so interesting about those Canadian geese?" he asked, annoyed at having to share her, even with a pair of feathered bipeds.

"Their loyalty," she said, her eyes confronting his. "They mate for life."

The hidden meaning in her words didn't escape him, but the return of the waitress with their orders prevented him from arguing the point. He now turned his attention to the lobster and the wine bottle. With each glass of wine she noticed that his glib tongue lost more of its sharpness.

Although the scrod was excellent, she ate only a few bites of it. She regretted her decision to meet him and was now anxious to bring their brief encounter to a swift end. Sitting across from him, she wondered what qualities could ever have drawn her to him in the first place. She had mistaken his arrogance for charm; his pomposity, for a way with words; his need to dominate others, for a genuine concern about his fellow man. Now a smile crossed her lips as she recalled Ned's humorous words about him: *"I know there couldn't possibly be a romance between you and Whitman. He's incapable of loving anybody but himself."*

"What's so amusing?" Roger asked, intruding upon her thoughts.

"Nothing," she said, watching the sun slip beneath the horizon.

As the meal dragged on, she fidgeted nervously but managed to be polite. Roger was working on the third bottle of wine, and she thought the dessert would never come. When finally the chocolate mousse arrived, he ate it too slowly to suit her. Glancing at her watch for the hundredth time, she finally could stand it no longer. "Your flight leaves at eleven-thirty," she reminded him.

Once again he looked at her with his insufferable vanity, saying, "You're still sounding very much like a staff aide concerned with my schedules and meetings. Are you sure you wouldn't consider returning to your old job?"

"No thanks," she swiftly replied.

"I can always be prevailed upon to catch a later flight out, you know," he said.

"There will be no need for that," she assured with finality as she arose.

"I'm getting the distinct impression you're not exactly thrilled to see me." He threw his napkin down on the table to emphasize his displeasure.

Outside a blend of darkness and fog shrouded everything. Only the sound of the peepers broke the eerie silence, and Julie sensed they were shouting shrill warnings to her. At the sight of her sports car, barely visible under the glow of a street lamp, Roger said, "I hope this time you'll at least allow me the honor of driving. I've never driven a Porsche."

"I thought there was nothing you hadn't done," she said, unable to resist the taunt.

"Not quite," he replied with a meaningful look.

She was so thankful that they would soon be on their way to the airport that she willingly handed him the keys. "Take the Ridge Road, it's unpaved but shorter," she said brusquely.

"Ah, but is it scenic and romantic?"

She just glared at him before settling into the passenger seat.

A mile down the highway he turned onto the graveled road, and she began to have misgivings about permitting him to drive. In the past whenever he drank to excess, his personality would change. Tonight was no exception. Gone was the cautious, conservative politician—replaced by an impulsive, reckless stranger. "I think you'd better let me drive," she said.

"Not until you agree to my terms," he replied with a silly grin.

"What terms?"

"Will you come back to work in my Washington office?"

"Of course not," she retorted, alarmed by his slurred speech.

Hearing her refusal, he pushed down on the accelerator.

"Slow down!" she admonished.

"Only when you respond positively to me," he insisted, turning his glazed eyes toward her.

"Please pay attention to the road," she told him, clutching the door handle.

Ignoring her suggestion, he said, "Will you marry me?"

"Don't be ridiculous."

"Maybe some mood music will help change your mind," he said, turning on the radio.

"For heaven's sake, Roger, slow down!"

"Not until you agree to marry me," he said.

"Never!" she gasped.

"Are you sure?" he asked, his foot pressing the gas pedal all the way to the floor and rocketing the Porsche along the graveled road.

"Stop this car immediately!" she cried.

That command came too late. On the turn above Jones Brook he lost control of the car, plunging it over the steep embankment. Julie could hear the branches of trees and underbrush scraping against its sides like mysterious hands reaching out to grasp her. "Oh, no!" she shrieked, recalling with horror the way her mother had died. "Not me too—"

Julie was unaware that Ned Baxter's van had pulled to a stop on the shoulder of the road above. Weary from his daily routine of writing, he had come to do some night fishing. Now he thought his headlights had caught the solitary figure of a man in the distance, scurrying across the field and disappearing among the trees. Were his eyes playing tricks on him, he wondered, rubbing them in an attempt to improve his vision.

Although nothing moved in front of him now, music wafted up from below, and a faint light glimmered through the fog. "Partyers here at this time of night!" he muttered, knowing that the town rowdies often gathered on certain desolate stretches of beach to break open and drain their six-packs.

But their being out here didn't make any sense to him. Where had they parked their cars, he asked himself. There were none to be seen along the edge of the road. He thought of finding another fishing spot but quickly dismissed the idea. This stream was his favorite. Besides, he reasoned, a short walk along its meandering banks would put a safe distance between him and the intruders. "I've come to fish and fish I will," he murmured with firm resolve. Shutting off the engine, he picked up his fishing gear and took out a flashlight from the glove compartment. Outside he followed its beam down a narrow path through the thick underbrush. The music grew louder. At the edge of the stream off to the right he saw the headlights of a car shimmering through the fog. "Oh, no!" he exclaimed, realizing it must have rolled down from above.

As he approached more closely, he could hear the engine running as the music blared. The door on the driver's side was ajar.

Dropping his fishing pole and tackle box, he reached in, fumbled for the key, and shut off the ignition, silencing the engine and radio. Now only the singing of crickets and croaking of frogs pierced the silence of the night.

As his eyes followed the beam of the flashlight across the interior of the Porsche, he recoiled at the sight of the young blonde slumped, unconscious, across the passenger seat. "Julie Hartwell!" he gasped.

A feeling of panic swept over him as he bent over and felt her pulse. "Thank heavens, she's alive," he whispered. He backed out of the car and stood up, nervously running a hand through his hair before he turned around resolutely and leaned back inside. Reaching across the seat, he brushed aside the torn seat belt and lifted Julie out of the car.

Cradling her protectively in his arms, he made his way carefully back up the steep incline. Except for the swelling on the side of her head, hidden by strands of hair, her face was unmarked. With her closed eyes, delicate features, and soft lips bathed in the faint glow of the moon and stars, she reminded him of a sleeping princess. In a moment of weakness he almost yielded to the temptation to kiss her, as if the touch of his lips, like that of some fabled Prince Charming, might arouse her magically from her deep slumber.

Upon reaching the road above, he placed her gently on the rear seat of his van. Rolling up his jacket, he set it under her head and shoulders. Then he covered her with a spare blanket. Satisfied that she was ready for the journey, he climbed behind the steering wheel and turned on the motor. Soon the van was streaking down the winding road toward the hospital. Once on the main highway, he found himself constantly glancing back at her. After what seemed an eternity, the vehicle pulled up in front of the emergency entrance of the hospital.

As he burst through the front door with her limp form in his arms, he called to the first person he saw, "This woman's been hurt in an automobile accident. She's unconscious and needs immediate attention."

Within seconds a nurse and an orderly had put Julie on a stretcher and were wheeling her into the emergency room. Julie didn't hear anything—not even the voice of the officious admitting clerk, who motioned Ned over to the reception desk to complete some forms and said, "Now tell me, young man, what's your wife's name?"

Chapter Eight

The pain in Julie's head was agonizing, and she was perspiring profusely. Her vision was blurred and she could only make out shadowy figures lurking around her. Just when she was beginning to think she must have died, her eyes focused and she realized she was in an emergency room. A bearded stranger, wearing a white jacket and brandishing a stethoscope, hovered over her. "How are you feeling?" he asked.

"Terrible," she moaned.

"Where's the pain?"

"The top of my head feels as if it's coming off," she complained, gingerly touching her temple.

"Do you know where you are?"

"In the hospital, obviously." Her tone left no doubt about her annoyance at the foolishness of the question.

"Yes. You're at Mount Pleasant Hospital, and I'm Dr. Bird."

She found herself wondering why anyone would name a hospital Mount Pleasant. As for the doctor's questions, she knew they were aimed at trying to find out the effects of her injury, but she still wished this Bird would fly away. Before she could tell him to do so, he asked another: "Can you tell me the color of my eyes?"

They were green like the senator's, prompting her to murmur, "What's happened to Roger?"

"Who's Roger?" he replied.

When she didn't answer, a voice in the background said, "She must be hallucinating."

"Yes," the doctor agreed. "All I know is that she was found alone in her car."

She wanted to sit up and scream that it was a lie, but she lacked even the strength to make that simple move. Her eyelids drooped, and she felt herself once again slipping into an exhausted sleep.

Faintly she could hear the doctor lecturing others—probably interns, she thought. "*Commotri cerebri,* commonly referred to as a brain concussion. Symptoms include a loss of consciousness, dizziness, visual dislocation, and cold perspiration. . . ."

In the morning, she was awakened by sunlight streaming through a corner window and reflecting off the waxed floor and pastel-colored walls. Glancing around the room, she noticed that the other bed was unoccupied. With great effort she managed to prop up her pillow and pull herself up against it. Touching the tender spot at the side of her head, she winced. Still, the pain had subsided and she was feeling better.

"*She was found alone in her car,*" the doctor had said. Now those words haunted Julie. Her concern for Roger's safety had changed to anger at him. Not only had his reckless driving caused the accident but it also had almost taken her life. After much reflection, she came to one inescapable conclusion: He must have thought she was dead. He had fled the scene in panic, hoping to protect his precious political future.

She could hardly wait to tell the police exactly what had happened. The whole world would soon find out just how noble Senator Roger Whitman really was. A vengeful smile crossed her face as she envisioned the headline of the *Washington Banner:* PROMINENT UNITED STATES SENATOR RUNS—FROM SCENE OF ACCIDENT.

Suddenly she remembered her father's promotion. Any such revelation to the police would certainly ruin his chances of becoming the next chief executive officer and might even jeopardize his current job as comptroller. Ever since the death of his wife and Julie's absence from home, Acme Electronics had become his whole life. She shuddered to think what might become of him if he lost his job. No, she decided, she wouldn't risk hurting him by exposing the senator's less-than-heroic actions.

Besides, she rationalized further, the accident had revealed Roger's true character. Right now she just wanted to be rid of him once and for all. She was certain he would never dare to show his face to her again. Most important of all, she felt thankful to be alive.

"I bet you're hungry." The friendly voice interrupting her train of thought came from a slight, bespectacled nurse standing at the foot of her bed.

"That's putting it mildly," Julie replied enthusiastically. "I'm so hungry even you look edible."

With a chuckle the nurse said, "Dr. Bird gave me strict orders to get you up and walking around as soon as you awoke. After that, I promise to get you some breakfast."

Before Julie could respond, the nurse was helping her ease her legs over the edge of the bed. With difficulty Julie arose, swaying slightly.

"Very good," the nurse said. "Now you know how the Leaning Tower of Pisa must feel."

Julie couldn't help but smile.

"Come on," the nurse said coaxingly. "Lean on me and try to take a few steps."

Supported by her arm, Julie surprised even herself by walking once around the room.

"Let's not overdo a good thing," the older woman cautioned, leading her back to the bed. Tucking her patient safely under the covers, she said, "Now I'm going to get you some orange juice and toast."

"I guess beggars can't be choosy," Julie replied.

At her lack of enthusiasm, the nurse said cheerily, "Tomorrow you'll be able to choose your meals from the menu." Then she disappeared, returning a short while later with a tray, which she carefully placed before Julie. As she turned to leave again, she said, "Oh, by the way, I told that nice young man you were going to be just fine."

"Young man?" Julie asked curiously.

"Yes. The one who saved your life. Ned—" She paused, unable to remember.

"Baxter?" Julie suggested incredulously.

"Yes. That's him," she replied. "If he hadn't arrived in the nick of time at the accident scene, I'm afraid you'd have been a goner."

Her revelation shocked Julie, who gasped, "I had no idea."

"You were in no condition to notice anything. Apparently he was doing some night fishing in Jones Brook and just happened to stumble upon your car." With a mischievous wink she added, "Although he didn't get any fish, he caught you."

While Julie was turning crimson, she added, "Now eat your food and get plenty of rest. That way you'll be out of here in no time." With those words she vanished through the doorway.

Munching on the toast and sipping at the juice, Julie could only marvel at the strange turn of events.

The next day she underwent a series of routine medical tests. Meanwhile the pain continued to ease and her strength was returning rapidly. Over her strenuous objections the doctor insisted that she remain in the hospital a few more days for further observation. Despite his warnings not to overtax herself, she spent most of her time out of bed and walking around the room and halls.

One evening she was sitting on the edge of the bed, leafing through a fashion magazine, when there was a knock on the door. "Come in," she said, putting the magazine aside. She looked up and exclaimed, "Ned Baxter! I don't believe it!"

"It's me, all right," he said. "I hope you're not sorry to see me."

As their eyes met, they smiled at each other. After an awkward silence, she said, "What I meant to say was that it's strange that you, of all people, should have found me at the bottom of the embankment."

"I told you once that the fates were trying to tell us something," he said.

"So you did," she agreed, recalling his parting words at their last meeting.

"You're looking much better." He studied her face unhurriedly, feature by feature.

She could tell by the sparkle in his hazel eyes that he was pleased with what he saw.

"I feel fine," she assured him. Self-conscious at his continuing scrutiny, she asked, "Is something the matter?"

"I was just thinking back to the night of your accident," he answered, his hand caressing the metal frame at the foot of her bed.

"Oh?" He had aroused her curiosity, for she couldn't remember anything that had happened after the car had plunged down the embankment.

"Do you realize that was the first time you and I met without getting into an argument?" His face broke into a grin that sent her pulses soaring.

"I'm afraid I can't take any credit for that," she replied, returning his smile. "I was hardly in a position to argue with you."

"I prefer you this way," he said. His expression grew serious as he added, "That's a dangerous road to take at night, especially when it's foggy and you're traveling alone."

His emphasis on the last word made her uneasy. It was almost as if he knew Roger had been in the car with her. She moved swiftly to change the subject, saying, "I didn't know you lived in Paradise Cove."

"In the past I've spent several summer vacations here. Despite an attempt on my life last year by someone whose name escapes me," he said teasingly, "I liked what I saw and decided to make it my permanent residence."

Blushing as she recalled their first encounter, she said, "I hope you didn't move here just to try to get even with me."

"No, the truth is that I'm an avid fisherman and there's plenty of opportunity here for both fresh- and salt-water fishing. I also wanted a place with some solitude where I could do my writing. And, of course, the natural beauty of the place is unsurpassed. Since the Jenkins property was for sale at a reasonable price, I jumped at the chance to buy it."

"No wonder I didn't see you anymore at the congressional library," she blurted out.

"If I'd known you cared, I'd have sent you my forwarding address."

While she was considering her next response, a bell rang to signal an end to the visiting hours.

"'At my back I always hear / Time's winged chariot hurrying near,'" he said with a sigh.

The quote brought a smile to her lips. "I see you're a fan of the English poet Andrew Marvell," she said.

"Yes." He seemed pleased that she could identify the writer of the verse. "I can't remember the title of that poem, but it's one of my favorites."

"I believe the title is 'To His Coy Mistress.' "

"Of course," he replied. "Freud would have something to say about me."

She also had some thoughts on what that eminent psychiatrist might say about him, but she chose not to reveal them. Besides, from his mischievous look she was beginning to get the feeling that his lapse of memory might have been intentional.

"You see," he told her, "we do have a lot in common, after all."

Those words contained more truth than she cared to admit, for she could feel an invisible web of attraction building between them. "Again, I want you to know how much I appreciate what you did for me," she said, extending her hand. "That night I was very lucky you happened along."

"Not as lucky as I was," he replied, eagerly accepting her hand.

They held hands for a moment before he released hers and walked to the door, where he paused to say, "I hope our paths will cross again—under happier circumstances, of course." Then, with a smile and a wave, he was gone.

"So do I," she whispered after him, the excitement of his touch still tingling throughout her.

That weekend Dr. Bird told Julie that the tests indicated she was suffering no ill aftereffects, and he agreed to release her from the hospital. "Since you did suffer a severe cerebral contusion and were unconscious for such a long time, I had to be certain there were no signs of edema or hemorrhage," he explained. "For the next month I must ask you to take things easy and avoid any kind of strenuous activity."

She acquiesced with a desultory nod. At this point she would have consented to anything just to get out of the place. Once she was in the taxicab and heading for The Gull's Way, a gleeful smile crossed her lips.

When she arrived there, she delighted in breathing in the good salt air. Finally she ambled across the lawn to the back of the house where, for a long time, she watched a distant figure hauling traps in a lobster boat on the whitecapped water. Climbing the stairs to go inside, she murmured, "It's good to be home."

In the days that followed, the salt air and lovely view proved more wholesome than anything the doctor might have prescribed. As she grew stronger, she found herself obeying her natural instincts, and sauntering along solitary stretches of the sandy white beach and sailing across the shimmering surface of the bay once again became important parts of her routine.

Often during such activities her thoughts would turn to Ned Baxter. Two weeks had passed since her release from the hospital. All that time she had hoped in vain for a telephone call from him. So Friday morning as the sun was climbing rapidly, promising a fine day, she decided to make the first move. She mounted her bicycle and soon was pedaling through the pine grove leading up to his cabin.

Unaware of her presence, Ned was typing away on his screened porch. The way his long fingers moved effortlessly across the keys told her that his creative juices were flowing. She suddenly felt guilty about intruding upon his writing time, and she was on the verge of silently pedaling away when he happened to glance up. "This is a pleasant surprise," he said enthusiastically, quickly shifting his attention from the typewriter to her.

"I hope I'm not interrupting your work," she said, pleased by his warm greeting.

"No, not at all," he assured her, rising. "Writing's fun, but typing's a drag."

"I thought all writers wrote on word processors nowadays," she said good-naturedly.

"I prefer to use 'Old Faithful' here," he replied, giving the typewriter an affectionate pat. "With me old habits die hard."

His long, lingering glance suggested that he'd like for her to become one of those old habits. "I came to thank you for what you did the night of the accident," she said, feeling a need to justify her visit.

"I'm glad you're here," he said with a smile that made her knees suddenly go weak. "I was just about to break for lunch." He pointed across the tree-lined yard to a barbecue grill whose coals were turning white hot. "Will you join me?"

"I'd be delighted," she replied, trying not to appear too eager. "What's the menu of the day?"

"How does shish kebab sound?"

"Oh, you don't have to go to all that bother," she protested.

"I insist," he replied, holding the screened door open for her. "The lamb's already been cut. Come inside while I get it."

The interior of the cabin was an airy, well-lit room with a sleeping loft accessible by a ladder. On the wall opposite the sink and refrigerator was the writing nook he had fashioned, complete with a desk, chair, and bookcase. The rest of the space was used as a living room, Spartanly furnished with a small sofa, a floor lamp, a few chairs, and some scatter rugs. Julie concluded that, like its occupant, the cabin was practical and unpretentious. "It's quaint," she said in obvious approval.

"I'm glad you like it," he said, glancing up from the skewers onto which he began placing the cubes of meat he had taken from the refrigerator.

Above his desk the photograph of a smiling, middle-aged woman in a vegetable garden caught her attention. "I bet this is your mother," she said, studying it intently.

"How'd you know?" he asked, arranging some vegetables on a platter.

"You have her smile."

He chuckled as he reached into a cabinet for cups, plates, and knives and forks, all of which he placed on a tray in front of him.

"She reminds me of my mother."

Her wistful tone caused him to look up and ask, "Is your mother dead?"

She nodded.

"I'm sorry to hear that."

With a shrug of resignation she said, "She also liked to putter around in her garden."

"Is your dad as nice as you?" he asked, adding some napkins and a salt shaker to the other items on the tray.

"More so," she said jokingly.

"In that case, maybe I'll fix him up with my mom," he said.

"Aren't you afraid you might be rushing things?"

He pursed his lips thoughtfully before admitting, "You're right. Besides, she'd be a challenge for any man." At her expression of surprise, he explained, "Don't get me wrong. I'm very fond of her and we get along well. It's just that she's a dynamo who's constantly got to be doing something. I guess I'm more laid-back and introspective. When she comes here for her annual visit, maybe I can introduce the two of you." He picked up the skewers and the platter. "If you'll take the tray and that empty pot, we'll go outside and begin the banquet celebration."

"Celebration?" she asked.

"Yes, it's great to see you're out of the hospital and looking so well. Frankly, I wanted to call you there and offer to drive you home, but I didn't have the nerve," he confessed. "After our past encounters, I'm afraid I've become gun-shy."

While he was placing the kabobs and vegetables on the grill, she set two places on the picnic table. "What made you decide to leave that center of the political universe on the banks of the Potomac?" she asked, sitting down on a bench.

"Truthfully, I was never very comfortable in Washington." A puff of smoke enveloped his sturdy frame as the flames from the charcoal licked at the oil oozing from the kabobs. "The pomp and pageantry of the place turned me off. Power was always the name of the game there."

She found herself nodding in agreement.

"Every social event, with its diplomats, government officials, ranking military officers, and movie stars, had an underlying motive—raising money, hailing a head of state, or praising some cause," he continued. "The inane conversation always was concerned with who's in and who's out."

His eloquent frankness struck a sensitive chord within her. "And how do you like it here?" she asked.

"Great," he replied, forgetting the grill momentarily and looking at her admiringly. "It has everything I could ever want."

The hidden meaning in both his look and his words didn't escape her.

He turned the skewers, saying, "And how did you find this place so aptly named Paradise Cove?"

"Ever since I can remember, my family has summered here."

"You were fortunate."

"Yes. I'll always cherish those memories."

"When will you be going back to Washington?" he said matter-of-factly as he moved the vegetables around on the grating with tongs.

She swallowed hard and blurted out, "Never."

What she had said made him drop the tongs.

As he stooped to pick them up, she added emphatically, "For the very reasons you've just stated, I, too, decided Washington wasn't for me. So I quit my job."

He stared at her wordlessly.

"Does that shock you?" she asked.

"It sounds almost too good to be true."

She raised her hand as if about to take an oath as she replied, "I'll swear to it if you'd like."

"I'm surprised that Roger agreed to let you go."

"I didn't know I needed his approval," she said, irritated at the mention of his name.

"It's just that I thought you and he were—" He paused, searching for the right words.

"Good friends?" she suggested.

"Something like that," he replied, accepting her choice of words with reluctance.

"I worked for the senator as a staff aide—nothing more, nothing less," she reminded him.

His eyes fell once again to the grill. "I guess the kabobs are done," he said with a shrug.

She breathed a sigh of relief to be off the odious topic of Roger Whitman. Soon she began to relax again. The aroma of the sizzling kabobs, mingling with the scent of the pines and salt air, gave her a heady feeling. She watched in fascination as Ned, with the touch of a master chef, cut the meat off the skewers and stirred them into a pot with the vegetables. "Dinner is served," he announced with a flourish as he set it on the picnic table.

Sitting across from each other, they stuffed half-moon-shaped pockets of Syrian bread with a mixture of sizzling kabobs and juicy vegetables. At the first bite she exclaimed, "This is delicious!"

"My mother always said that someday I'd make some lucky woman a good cook." His hazel eyes flashed a gentle but firm hint that she just might be that lucky person.

They spent the rest of the afternoon chatting amiably about a host of topics ranging from where to go for the best pizza in town to how to end the threat of nuclear war. For the first time since they had met, she felt completely at ease with him—almost as if she had known him all her life. And when their conversation dwindled into silence, she enjoyed the pleasant sensation of just sitting across from him.

As the charcoal embers were burning lower and the shadows cast by the tall fir trees were lengthening, his features hardened and he appeared lost in thought, prompting her to ask, "Is something wrong?"

He regarded her with a somber curiosity. "I have a couple of questions I'd like to ask you."

"Go ahead," she said with a sense of foreboding.

Taking a deep breath, he asked, "Do you

know that Roger Whitman owns a lot of stock in Acme Electronics?"

The question hit her hard. "I could hardly care less what he does," she replied, upset that Ned was leading her back to a subject she loathed.

Although she could tell he was affected by her strong negative reaction, this time he refused to back off. "A senator on the Armed Services Committee isn't supposed to be channeling contracts to a company in which he has a financial interest," he persisted. "It's a matter of ethics."

"I'm afraid ethics aren't a high priority with Roger," she said with a scornful laugh.

"It's not him I'm concerned about," he answered, the lines on his brow deepening. "It's your father."

"But I'm sure he's done nothing wrong," she said, rushing to his defense.

"Isn't he the comptroller of the company?"

"Yes." Her eyes narrowed suspiciously. "You seem to know a lot about him."

"In case you've forgotten, I used to be an investigative reporter," he reminded her. "The problem is that if Roger's financial wheeling and dealing comes under close public scrutiny, so will the actions of the management at Acme—including those of your father."

Her body tensed up, and she felt ill at the thought of discussing the senator again. And as for her father, she didn't even want to think about the implications of any wrongdoing on his part. Eager to move on to another subject, she stammered, "You said you had another question."

"Yes." He hesitated, and she sensed he was trying to get up the courage to ask it. "You weren't driving the Porsche the night of the accident, were you?" he said accusingly.

She froze. Finally she managed to reply, "How could you ask such a thing?"

"When I reached the car that night, you were slumped across the passenger seat." His eyes were searching her face for some reaction. "One strap of the seat belt had torn loose from the anchor bolt on the floor—caused by the impact of the accident, I assume."

"What if I told you that belt's been broken for a long time?" she shot back.

"Then I'd suggest you use the other one whenever you get behind the wheel," he replied.

"And I'd advise you to have a whistle and a flotation device on board your skiff the next time you go fishing out on the bay," she retorted.

"Touché," he said with a nod of his head.

In her anger all his motives now became suspect. He cared nothing about her or her father, she thought. His sole interest was to gather spicy new tidbits for inclusion in his book. "I knew your truce wouldn't last," she shouted, rising. "If you have any other questions about the accident, I suggest you go to the police station and read the report I filed there." She hurried toward her bicycle.

He was on his feet, pursuing her. "I hardly think the local police are infallible," he replied, overtaking her with his long strides. "Besides, I want to know whom you're protecting."

Mounting her bicycle, she fired a verbal shot back at him. "I've managed to put the horror of that night behind me, and I don't intend to discuss it with you or anybody else."

Placing his hand on the bicycle frame to prevent her from moving, he asked, "Why must you always run away when things don't go your way?"

"Because it's difficult for me to defend myself against a man who's saved my life." Her tears quickly put an end to his interrogation and he released his grip. "No matter what you may think of me, I want you to know I appreciate what you did the night of the accident," she said, struggling not to cry. Then she turned away from him to hide her tears and put all her frustration into pedaling homeward.

Julie was pedaling at a furious pace, trying to put as much distance as possible between herself and the source of her anger—Ned Baxter. When she wasn't berating herself for her folly in going to see him, she was reliving all the recent events leading up to the debacle at the cabin.

It had all started with his visit to the hospital. At the time she could feel what she thought was a growing attraction between them. "*I told you the fates were trying to tell us something,*" he had said. She, too, had believed they were fated to meet. Why else had he happened along in time to save her? Foolishly, she had even imagined that their relationship could blossom into a more positive and meaningful one.

Upon her release, his curly hair, hazel eyes, and disarming smile had become her obsession. During that week at The Gull's Way, how many times had she found herself glancing impatiently at the telephone, hoping in vain to hear from him? When she could no longer tolerate his absence, she had come up with a convenient pretext to see him: She had to go and thank him personally for saving her life. What a colossal mistake!

Reluctantly she had to admit that their afternoon together had been one of the most idyllic and enjoyable of her life. But just when she was sure of their mutual warmth and affection for each other, he had to go and ruin it all.

She knew she had a short temper. In the past her father had often reminded her tactfully of that flaw. But this time her anger was justified. *Ned and his darn questions,* she fumed. He had no right to probe and accuse. The instincts of the investigative reporter ran too deeply in his veins. He would never change. To him, both she and her father were simply the means to get a good story.

Now she had a good idea who the main character in that story was. From the beginning Ned's disdain for the senator had been apparent. Hadn't he delighted in belittling him at the meeting of defense contractors? There could be no doubt about it, he was hell-bent on destroying Roger's political career. If Ned had to use her and her father to accomplish that end, so be it.

It was ironic that she now found herself in the unenviable position of defending the senator. Only her devotion to her father and her fear of hurting his chances for the promotion blunted any expression of her own loathing for Roger and prevented her from revealing his cowardly behavior the night of the accident.

Then, of course, there was Ned's book, *Washington Payola.* Naturally he'd fill it with juicy morsels about political deceit and corruption in the nation's capital. Although Roger was obviously at the top of his hit list, everyone became fair game—including her father and her. The more scandalous the revelations, the better. Wasn't that the way books were sold today? As an aspiring young writer, Ned surely had hopes of making the best-seller list.

She bristled, suddenly feeling that Ned had wined and dined her solely in the hopes of getting information about the senator and her father. He would get nothing from her, she swore to herself, absolutely nothing.

When she reached The Gull's Way, she was still fuming—so she changed into her bathing suit, grabbed a towel, and headed for the beach to try to cool off in the most literal sense. No sooner had she started across the lawn than she heard the noise of wheels turning on the graveled driveway. It was Ned's van. Slowly he climbed out and ambled toward her with his head bowed and his hands thrust deeply into the pockets of his denim jeans. Despite his contrite demeanor, she couldn't resist asking sarcastically, "To what do I owe the honor of this visit?"

He halted abruptly several yards from her, stunned by the sight of her in a yellow bikini that alluringly revealed the splendid proportions of her body. Self-consciously she draped the towel across her shoulders, bringing him quickly back to the purpose of his visit. "I've come to apologize," he mumbled, nervously running a hand through his hair. "If I said anything back at the cabin that hurt you, I'm sorry. It's just that when something's on my mind, I have to get it off."

"Lately you must have a lot on your mind. You seem to be having trouble holding your head up." With that caustic retort she brushed past him and started down the wooden steps to the beach below.

"Hey!" he called after her. "Are you accepting my apology or not?"

Halfway down, she turned and replied, "As I've said before, it's hard to refuse someone who's just saved your life."

"Forget that lifesaving business, will you?" he said, miffed at her mocking tone.

She smiled at his discomfort.

"Do you mind if I tag along?" he asked.

"It's a public beach, but I'm sure you won't find any political tidbits for your book down there," she said tauntingly.

While he stood above, shaking his head at her gibe, she turned and once again moved toward the crescent-shaped shoreline. When she reached the white sand, in one smooth motion she dropped the towel and kicked off her sandals. Before Ned reached the last step, she was in the water.

With steady overhand strokes Julie swam toward a distant float. Already the refreshing coolness of the salt water was working its magical powers. The nervous tension was subsiding, and her taut muscles were relaxing. She rolled over on her back, her feet still propelling her ahead. A sidelong glance caught the sight of Ned standing on shore with crossed arms and a pained expression. A faint smile played around the edges of her mouth, for she was pleased that he had cared enough to apologize. Perhaps there was hope for him after all, she thought.

With a frown Ned sat down and resigned himself to picking up and releasing handfuls of sand. He glanced up and watched as she pulled her supple body onto the raft. When she lay down on the wooden decking with her delicate features and bent knees raised to the adoring sun, he couldn't take it anymore. He leaped to his feet. Kicking away his shoes and tearing off his shirt, he lunged through the incoming tide and began swimming toward her.

As he hauled himself, dripping wet, onto the float, she took her hand away from her eyes long enough to inspect him. "Do you know you've just ruined a perfectly good pair of jeans?" she said coolly.

Suddenly his mood turned buoyant. "I happen to think you're worth the sacrifice."

Fighting off the effects of his warm smile, she said, "Flattery will get you nowhere." Again she shielded her eyes from the sun and proceeded to ignore him.

He lay down on his side with his head propped up on his elbow, facing her. For a long time the only sounds were the lapping of the waves against the sides of the raft and the plaintive call of a circling gull.

Petulantly his voice broke the silence.

"Look, Jewel," he complained, "we can't go on this way."

Once again she looked at him frostily. "For your information, my name is Julie."

"To me, you're much too precious to be called anything but Jewel," he said.

She stared at him in disbelief. "You're really something! First you've ruined a perfectly wonderful morning by making all kinds of innuendos about my father and me—not to mention grilling me like a kabob on your barbecue. Then you have the nerve to follow me here. Now you've taken it upon yourself to change my name." Though she struggled to maintain a stern expression, she couldn't prevent a smile from breaking through.

Ignoring her litany of his crimes, he turned his grin up another notch. "I really do prefer you when you're smiling."

"You're impossible," she said, trying without success to look serious. "I could think of a dozen nicknames to call you, but I promised my beloved mother I'd never use profanity."

They exchanged smiles before she lay back and once again closed her eyes, unwilling to fall victim to his charm. For a long time she lay motionless, dozing under the rays of the sun and lulled by the gentle swaying of the float.

She had no idea that the sight of her was renewing all the emotions he had felt the night he had plucked her from the car and carried her to safety. Even then he had been seized with the desire to kiss her. Only his concern for her well-being had prevented it. Had she opened her eyes now, she would have seen a similar longing on his face, and this time it wouldn't be denied.

He leaned over and brushed his lips against hers. As he drew back, warily testing her reaction to the liberty he had just taken, her eyelids opened. To his relief, all traces of her earlier anger were gone. "Again, I'm sorry if I offended you back at my place." He spoke softly but with deep conviction.

For Julie, the kiss was a source of indescribable pleasure. As she looked up into his hazel eyes, she murmured, "Why must we always end up fighting?"

"I was just about to ask you that same question." His voice had more confidence now.

"Are you implying it's all my fault?" she asked, raising an eyebrow.

"You do tend to get upset easily over things."

"My father's reputation happens to be very important to me," she said.

"See." He threw his arms up into the air as a sign of his frustration. "There you go again. This time I refuse to be drawn into another argument."

"So I'm an imperfect human being." In her

tone was a grudging admission that he just might be right about her emotional makeup.

Looking down at her again with amused affection, he said, "If anything, you're perfection personified." After a long pause during which they gazed into each other's eyes, he asked, "Have you accepted my apology?"

"How do I know it was genuine?" she asked teasingly.

He bent over and kissed her once again. "Now do you believe me?"

"I have to," she replied, unable to conceal her happiness. "Your kiss is even more persuasive than your smile. I accept your apology."

"Great." His face was still poised above hers. "Now I want to declare a permanent truce between us."

Her eyes sparkled. "No, this time I demand your unconditional surrender."

"Then you shall have it," he whispered.

As his lips pressed hers for the third time, she closed her eyes, savoring their touch and losing all track of time. His soft voice coaxed her back to reality. "Are you okay?" he asked, leaning over her tenderly.

Raising her lids, she focused on his hazel eyes, aquiline nose, and firm mouth. "Yes," she said, her arms still around him, "but now you're my prisoner."

"And I'll remain so forever," he murmured,

caressing the salt-kissed tendrils of hair framing her face.

For a while they lay on their backs, gazing up at the white puffs of clouds skidding across the blue sky. Finally Ned broke the silence. "I want you to know I'd never do anything to hurt you or your father."

"I believe you," she said, reaching over to give him a reassuring pat.

"I've got a draft of my book in the van. It's for you."

"Why?"

"I want you to see for yourself that nowhere inside is there a word about your father—" He hesitated before adding, "Or Roger Whitman."

"You didn't have to do that. You've just convinced me how foolish I've been not to trust you." Reaching up and placing her fingers over his mouth, she murmured, "I just don't want to hear any more about all their problems."

"I understand." He leaned over and kissed her on the forehead, whispering, "I love you."

"It must be contagious because I feel the same way about you," she replied with a blissful sigh. "But tell me how much you love me."

"Enough to get you anything you want in the whole world."

"How about the moon this evening?" she said, playfully massaging his back.

"Is that an invitation to see you again?"

"Of course."

"In that case I'll bring along a ladder and some rope to haul it down for you."

In silence they lingered on the float, rocked gently by the undulation of the incoming tide and serenaded by the whispers of waves washing against the underside of the raft. A catamaran sailed past them, and they waved a return greeting to its occupants. "Now, that's the way to go through life, isn't it?" he said mischievously. "Twin hulls side by side."

"Yes," she answered with a knowing smile, "it has definite advantages."

When she arose reluctantly, he asked, "Where are you going?"

With a heavy sigh, she said, "All good things must come to an end."

"Come on now," he chided, looking up at her. "Let's think positively. I'm certain many more such delightful afternoons await us."

"Is that a promise?"

"Cross my heart and hope to die if I ever tell a lie."

She laughed. "Now I want to see just how resourceful you really are. I'll race you to shore."

Before he could reply, she sliced through the surface of the water in a perfect dive. Hardly had her shapely legs disappeared below than her head emerged yards away from the float.

With a taunting smile she began to swim shoreward.

Unable to resist her challenge, he jumped to his feet and dived in after her. Though she was a good swimmer, his powerful overhand strokes soon brought him alongside her. Finishing the race in a dead heat, they struggled onto the beach. Flinging themselves down on the white sand, they broke into laughter. "I never thought you'd be able to catch me," she said breathlessly.

With a twinkle in his eyes, he replied, "Never underestimate my physical powers when I'm in pursuit of a mermaid."

Rising, they instinctively joined hands and strolled happily along the beach.

Chapter Nine

Julie hadn't seen her father since she had stopped by his house on her way from Washington to The Gull's Way. His kindness in giving her the summer property had brought tears of joy to her eyes. As soon as she had reached Paradise Cove, she had sat down and written him a deeply emotional thank-you letter in which she had expressed her appreciation for all the warmth and love both he and her mother had lavished upon her.

Since her release from the hospital, she had been trying to get up the courage to telephone him. There were several reasons for her reluctance. She knew he'd be upset with her for not telling him sooner about the accident, and she really wasn't looking forward to one of his benign scoldings.

At the time she hadn't wanted to worry him. Recently he had seemed more tense and nervous than usual. She suspected his change in mood had something to do with his concern about succeeding J. C. Trimble as president of Acme Electronics. Had she called him from the hospital, he would have raced down to be at her bedside, monitoring her every move. The only thing worse than a mother hen was a father rooster, she thought.

Then, of course, he'd want to know exactly how the mishap had occurred, opening up all her old wounds. Although his questions would come from the heart, still she would have to lie. Even though she concealed what had happened just to protect his job and enhance his chances for his coveted promotion, doing so was agonizing for her. If, by some chance, he were to find out why she was hiding the truth, his eyes would cloud over in sadness and he'd remind her, with carefully chosen words, that nothing could justify such a course of action—not even his own well-being.

Friday afternoon she was strolling along the shore below the house, eddies of retreating water teasing the soles of her bare feet, when the inevitable happened. Hearing someone calling her name, she turned around and saw the unmistakable figure of her father. He was waving his arms to catch her attention and hurrying toward her. "Oh, no!" she gulped, bracing herself for what she knew was surely to come.

When he caught up to her, he embraced her

warmly. But his rebuke came sooner than she had anticipated. "What do you mean by not notifying me of your accident?" he demanded.

"Since I was unconscious at the time, I could hardly call you, could I?" she said with a nervous giggle. "And when I awoke in the hospital, I felt fine. Besides, I didn't want you to get as upset as you are now."

Her words had a calming effect upon him. "I'd like to have Dr. Lawrence examine you," he said, studying her with the paternal concern that had exasperated her so often in the past.

For a successful and worldly businessman, her father was remarkably old-fashioned, she often felt. Now was one of those times. His invoking the name of the family doctor served only to remind her of a past dependency she had long since outgrown. "Dad, I've undergone all kinds of tests at the hospital, and I feel fine," she assured him.

With a sigh of resignation he backed off, saying, "Ever since you went to Washington, you've become too independent."

"I'm a big girl now," she reminded him gently.

"Yes, and I must admit I don't like it," he said, putting his arm around her shoulders in a conciliatory gesture. "Come on now, don't let me interrupt your afternoon stroll." He fell into step alongside her, asking, "Just what caused the accident?"

In the deep waters beyond the mouth of the bay, Julie spotted a freighter heading for Europe and, at that instant, she wished she were aboard it. If rehashing the events of that fateful night was painful, lying to her father was more so. "The car just went out of control on the road above Jones Brook. It's that simple."

"I can't understand it. You know that road so well." He scratched his head in bewilderment. "I hope you're not developing a heavy foot on the gas pedal whenever you get behind the wheel."

"Oh, Dad!" she exclaimed in exasperation.

At her derisive tone, he conceded, "I suppose I shouldn't dwell on it. The most important thing is that you're alive and looking well, considering the ordeal you've gone through." While she bent over to tease a fiddler crab that quickly scurried for cover, he asked, "What's happened to your car?"

"It's at the auto body shop for repairs. Other than some dents, a smashed grill, and a leaky radiator, it's in remarkably good condition."

"I'll have the station wagon sent up in the morning," he said.

"That won't be necessary. I have a bicycle—the French racer you bought especially for me. It'll get me wherever I want to go until my car's repaired. Besides, bicycling gives me a chance to lose some of the weight I put on in Washington."

He surveyed her over his glasses, saying, "Whatever happened to that girl of mine who loved fancy sports cars, yacht clubs, and foreign travel?"

"She's finally learned that the simple things in life are the most important."

"Name some," he challenged her good-naturedly.

She paused, stooping to pick up something. "Like finding a sand dollar," she replied, handing it to him. "Or just being here with you."

"I certainly can't argue with you on those points." His face broke out into a smile.

As they walked on, sometimes Julie would dash out playfully to meet the remains of an incoming wave and feel the refreshing coolness of the salt water swirling around her ankles. How many times as a child, she wondered, had she cavorted along that same stretch of sandy beach, indulging in similar antics while her mother and father looked on in amusement?

"Last week I ran into Roger Whitman," he said, picking up a flat stone whose edges had been rounded by the ceaseless churning of the tides.

The color vanished from her face at the mention of the name.

"He makes no secret of his fondness for you." He sent the stone skipping across the surface of the water, and she wished she could do the same thing with her memories of the senator. "I don't know what happened between the two of you," he said, watching the stone sink from sight, "but he's eager to repair the damage and get back together with you."

"I'm afraid that's impossible," she said, clenching her fists.

As he turned to face her, he appeared relieved, saying, "I'm glad you're beginning to show better taste in your choice of men. I think Ned Baxter's more your type."

Her eyes widened in astonishment. "How do you know him?"

"This morning he came to see me."

Julie had been so busy defending herself for not telling her father about the accident and fending off his questions about Roger, it never had occurred to her to ask him how he had found out about the mishap. But now she knew Ned was the culprit. Reeling in anger and shock, she blurted out, "The nerve of him!"

"Frankly, I'm glad he came," he said, reaching for a piece of driftwood. "The news of your accident just happened to slip out in the course of our conversation. I can assure you that your accident wasn't the reason for his visit."

"He should mind his own business," she said, fuming.

"When you're in love with someone, everything about that person becomes your business." He spoke nonchalantly as he examined the smoothness of the wood.

A scarlet flush overspread her features, and for a moment she was at a loss for words. "Just what was the purpose of his visit?" she finally asked, choosing to ignore his last comment.

"It had to do with Roger and Acme Electronics."

Still flustered by his frank appraisal of her relationship with Ned, she said, "What's that got to do with you?"

"A lot." He looked across the bay in an obvious attempt to avoid her eyes. "I have a confession to make. Do you remember when you last stopped over at the house and asked me about Roger's involvement with Acme?"

"Yes, of course."

"I wasn't being honest with you," he said, turning to face her. At her look of disappointment, he explained, "It wasn't so much that I lied to you as it was that I failed to tell you everything."

"As I recall," she said, raising an eyebrow, "at the time you did seem eager to change the subject."

"Since confession is good for the soul, I'd like to make a clean breast of it now." Taking a deep breath, he said, "Ned's doing research for a book—an exposé of political corruption in Washington."

"Yes, I know." There was a hint of impatience in her voice.

"A disgruntled former executive from Acme

by the name of Joe Ridley had telephoned him, hinting at political hanky-panky between Roger and the company. Joe's an unsavory character who'd do anything for the right price. Naturally he demanded money for the complete story."

"Ned would never stoop to that, would he?" Once again she found herself having serious doubts about Ned's motives.

"No, of course not," he assured her. "But he did set out to do some digging of his own. Unfortunately, what he found wasn't very good."

"What do you mean?"

"For some time the company's been supplying Roger with freebies, like the use of executive jets, legal consultation with company lawyers, speeches before a captive audience of plant workers, and, of course, jobs for his friends and relatives."

"From what I learned in my short stay in Washington, that's the norm for many politicians there."

"That still doesn't make it right," he pointed out. "Naturally Roger wasn't satisfied with all those perks. He wanted something else." He threw down the piece of driftwood, emphasizing his disgust.

"Money," she interjected intuitively.

He nodded. "Yes. And lots of it."

"That doesn't surprise me. He always said

'You can't buy an election with money, but you can substantially improve your chances.' "

"Last week the president of the company, J. C. Trimble, asked me to help form a PAC for Roger."

"A Political Action Committee?"

"Yes. He sees that as a convenient way of channeling money to a friendly politician whose influence has become most helpful in getting important government contracts for the company. After all, there isn't a large civilian market for our specialty—guidance systems for missiles and bomb sites."

"Aren't PACs limited to raising one thousand dollars per person and five thousand dollars per company?"

"Yes, but J.C. has a scheme to maximize company contributions. Whenever a worker receives any kind of promotion, J.C. plans to send a thousand dollars in that person's name to Roger's campaign."

"But that's illegal!" she exclaimed.

"Only if the authorities find out, and no one's going to be foolish enough to incur the wrath of the boss and jeopardize his or her job by complaining. Besides, as long as the employee gets the promotion and the hefty salary increase that goes along with it, what does he or she care?"

"If anything should happen, Roger and Trimble would be guilty of wrongdoing, not you." She was trying to convince herself almost as much as her father.

"I wish it were that simple," he said with a sigh of resignation. "Unfortunately, in my role as comptroller, I'm involved in all financial aspects of the company. That means I'll also be handling the PAC money."

"What can you do?"

"I suppose I could swallow my pride and go along with their plan. If it becomes public, I can always say I was only following Trimble's orders."

"That way you'd be able to get the promotion." Hope replaced the despair in her eyes. "Then when you're president, you can change the way things are done."

"Perhaps." His response was so lacking in conviction that she turned to him. He was staring out at the water, lost in thought.

"Isn't the promotion important to you anymore?" she asked.

With a shrug he quoted the Bible: " 'For what is a man profited, if he shall gain the whole world and lose his own soul?' "

As they walked on in silence, she thought she saw his eyes misting, and it broke her heart.

After that, Julie had an uneasy feeling about her father. Never in her life had she seen him so downcast and unhappy as he appeared on the day of his visit. She knew his job meant everything to him, and now it frightened her to think what might happen to him if he were to lose it. But if events forced him to choose between the company and his personal integrity, she had no doubt what choice he would make.

As for Ned, she was hurt that he had taken it upon himself to go see her father without telling her. But even now her father's words in defense of Ned's motives were ringing in her ears: "*When you're in love with someone, everything about that person becomes your business.*" Still, some doubts lingered in her mind.

So, despite her mixed feelings, she wasted no time in confronting Ned when they met that weekend. "What right did you have to go see my father?" she asked him accusingly, granting free rein to her pent-up emotions.

His eyes surveyed her critically as he said, "You still don't trust me, do you?"

"Sneaking around behind my back isn't exactly the way to go about building up trust," she replied with a frown.

The tensing of his jaw betrayed his underlying frustration. "Do you think I'm a crass opportunist in search of some spicy material for my book?"

"I don't know what to believe anymore." She spoke more in confusion than anger. "You might at least have told me you were going there. After all, he is my father."

"No matter what I do, I can't seem to win

with you," he said, throwing his hands up in the air. "You didn't want to hear anything about problems involving your father or—" He hesitated, choosing his words with care. "Or a certain politician. Even though it's been killing me, I've kept my word."

His veiled reference to the senator shook her. "I certainly wouldn't want to be responsible for your early demise," she replied sharply.

Brushing aside her sarcasm, he said, "Since I didn't dare say anything to you, I did the next best thing. I went to talk with your father."

"I know all about your conversation with him," she said, refusing to concede him anything.

His look of annoyance quickly passed. "At least *he's* able to communicate with you."

That mild rebuke raised her hackles. "Just what do you mean by that?" she asked.

"Merely that I envy him." He reached into his pocket and took out a handkerchief. As he waved it in a gesture of surrender, her frosty expression melted into a smile.

"I'm sorry," she said, feeling guilty for having lashed out at him.

He looked intently at her delicate features before he said mischievously, "I prefer a Jewel that sparkles."

She found herself smiling. "The last thing I want is an argument with you," she confessed, "but I'm really worried about Dad."

"I share your concern," he said softly. "No matter what you may think of me, I went only to warn him."

Suddenly she was ashamed of herself for doubting his motives. Even her father had taken her to task for harboring such negative sentiments.

"I heard about some shady dealings between Acme Electronics and that certain public official," he explained. "If true, they could have serious consequences for the officers of the company, including your father."

"He's done nothing wrong." She was trying to convince herself more than him.

"Up until now the company's walked a fine line between what's legal and illegal in supporting its favorite congressman."

At the hint of censure in his voice, she interjected, "Washington politicians are always careful to leave themselves loopholes big enough to drive trucks through."

"Yes, but now the president of the company is really stretching the bounds of propriety with his clever scheme to funnel money into a PAC."

Her face clouded with uneasiness. "I know. Dad told me about it."

"Not only is it unethical," he said, unable to restrain his feeling of outrage, "but it's illegal."

"But if Trimble is supporting it and Dad

doesn't go along—" She stammered, realizing that everything for which her father had worked so hard—particularly his chance to assume the presidency of the company—might now be in jeopardy. "It surely will mean the end of his career at Acme," she concluded in a hushed voice.

"That may be the price he has to pay for his integrity."

Riled by his attitude, she shot back, "That's easy for you to say."

"The company's become his whole life," he said, responding to the accusation in her words. "That's not healthy."

"I realize that," she admitted. "But I couldn't stand seeing him as depressed and unhappy as he was when he left here."

"Maybe we can help change that," he said, placing a reassuring hand on her arm.

His innate strength and self-confidence made her feel more secure. At his touch, a current of comfort coursed through her. She wanted to confide in him—to tell him everything that had happened the night of the accident—but she wavered.

Sensitive to her distress over her father, he chose to change the subject, saying nonchalantly, "Speaking of parents, I'm expecting my mother to arrive for a visit sometime next week. I'd like you to meet her."

"Yes, of course." In the past his good-natured kidding about some of his mother's faults had aroused her curiosity. So naturally Julie was eager to meet her.

The next Monday Mrs. Baxter arrived. Because of a phobia about flying, she had driven all the way out from California. That feat alone had impressed Julie. The tall, gray-haired woman with the boundless reserve of energy and the glib tongue was even more intimidating than Ned had implied.

While he was making the introductions, she was studying Julie with maternal intensity. "So you're the young lady who's stolen my son's heart!" she exclaimed. Then, with a smile that would have melted a banker's cold heart, she embraced Julie warmly. While Julie was being held in her bear hug, she glanced over her shoulder to find Ned wearing a similar grin. Julie was sure of two things: Mrs. Baxter approved of her, and Ned had definitely inherited his own potent smile from his mother.

Mrs. Baxter wasted no time in taking over the daily upkeep of the cabin. Julie quickly came to understand why Ned had looked upon the visit with mixed feelings. With her well-meaning assertiveness, his mother could be difficult to handle. She also was perpetual motion incarnate. Whenever Julie stopped by, Ned's mother had a spatula in one hand and a vacuum cleaner in the other. Although Ned was by no means a slovenly housekeeper, under her watchful eyes the interior of the cabin was transformed into a shiny and spotless showpiece. If she wasn't inside waxing floors or hanging curtains, she was outside mowing grass or planting flowers.

Prior to Mrs. Baxter's visit, Julie and Ned had settled into a certain routine. Because he was busy putting the finishing touches on his book during the week, they reconciled themselves to seeing each other on weekends. So Wednesday afternoon she was pleasantly surprised when he telephoned. In a bid to escape his doting mother for a while, he invited Julie to a movie that evening. For her, their long hours apart had proved irksome, and she was glad for the chance to see him, however briefly.

They went to a local movie house where a Woody Allen film was playing. In the darkness she relaxed against the back of her seat, enjoying the warm sense of security at Ned's presence. The scent of his after-shave lotion gave her a giddy feeling, entirely apropos for the comedy they were watching. Soon they both were rocking back and forth in outbursts of uproarious laughter at the actor's antics on screen. But for Julie, true happiness was just being by Ned's side, and, at that moment, because of his presence, all her worries about her father vanished.

Afterward, over coffee at a doughnut shop, he complained, "As much as I love my mother, she's already driving me up a wall. Whenever she comes here, she insists on treating me like a two-year-old. Her basic assumption is that I'm incapable of surviving on my own."

"Perhaps she's right," Julie said teasingly.

"That's not funny," he replied, trying to keep a straight face. "I'm a stranger in my own home, and she's a candidate for the Good Housekeeping Seal of Approval."

He got no sympathy from Julie, whose features showed clearly that she thought the whole thing was hilarious.

"Just look at me," he lamented, rubbing his stomach to emphasize his point. "I've already gained ten pounds, and I haven't been able to do a lick of work on my book."

"Don't you realize that's what mothers are for?" she asked lightly. "Besides, if you can't take some tender loving care from her, how are you ever going to cope with a warm, affectionate wife?" Those words just came tumbling out and she immediately regretted them.

"Is that a hint?" he asked, the corners of his mouth twitching in amusement.

She was too embarrassed to reply.

His eyes shone with a compelling twinkle as he said, "When the time comes, I'm sure I'll find a way to cope."

Regaining her poise, she said, "Cheer up, you have only a week and a half to survive."

A supportive squeeze of his arm accompanied the pep talk.

"Thanks, I needed that." He placed his hand on hers. "But I'm not sure I can last that long without your help. Will you do me a favor, Jewel?"

Although she had objected strenuously the first time he had used his pet name for her, now she never tired of hearing it. It was more than a term of endearment; it had become the password to her heart. "How could I possibly refuse when you've just said the magic word?" she asked.

"Will you invite your father to join the three of us for supper at Liam's Friday evening?"

She raised an eyebrow suspiciously. "Why, all of a sudden, are you playing Cupid?"

Undaunted, he replied, "Don't you think inviting your father would be a nice gesture on our part?"

She burst out laughing.

"What do you find so amusing?"

As she watched him struggle to look serious, she asked, "How come I'm getting the distinct impression you're trying to foist your mother off on my poor, unsuspecting father?"

Once again that familiar smile broke through his solemn facade. "Because it's the truth."

After their laughter subsided, he said, "Will you invite him?"

"I'll have to think about it," she said playfully.

"It's a matter of life and death," he told her with mock earnestness. "I warn you that the headlines in tomorrow's newspapers may read, *Mom Kills Son with Kindness.*"

She laughed. "I certainly wouldn't want that on my conscience. I'll invite him."

Julie worried about her father. His enthusiasm and zest for life were still missing, and he was agonizing over how best to handle the PAC problem. So she had gotten into the habit of calling him frequently to check on his well-being.

When during one such telephone call she invited him to the supper date, to her surprise he eagerly accepted. Since the death of his wife, he had never been out with another woman. It was almost as if he wanted Julie's approval before even thinking about such a social adventure.

That Friday he arrived at The Gull's Way earlier than expected. She was pleased to see him acting more like his old positive self. He spent the afternoon in one of the bedrooms preening for the big event. When finally he came out, Julie's eyes widened in approval at his blue suit, red tie, and leather shoes with—of all things—tassels. "How do I look?" he asked, turning playfully for her final inspection.

"Debonair and spiffy," she replied in amusement. "I'm going to be jealous at having to share you with Mrs. Baxter."

As the hour to go and pick up the others approached, she noticed he was growing more nervous. No sooner had they climbed into his Cadillac, which he had washed and polished for the occasion, than he jumped out and dashed back into the house. Soon he returned, carrying a dozen roses, a gift for Mrs. Baxter, which he had nearly forgotten.

When they arrived at the cabin, he hung sheepishly behind Julie. Ned drew him out, making the introductions. "Mr. Hartwell, this is my mother, Rose," he said.

Beaming, but more subdued than Julie had seen her previously, Mrs. Baxter was wearing a pleated pink dress that lent a royal quality to her tall, stately figure. "I'm delighted to meet you," she said, extending her hand.

"And I'm happy to meet you," he replied. He handed her the roses, saying, "I've brought these for you."

"Roses are my favorite," Mrs. Baxter said as she inhaled their fragrance.

"Roses for a Rose," he said with a nervous laugh.

"They're beautiful," she replied, putting them into a vase Ned brought her.

Inside the restaurant Julie was heartened to see her father so relaxed and cheerful. Throughout the meal he and Mrs. Baxter chatted amiably, at times oblivious to the presence of their children, who looked on with pleasure. Over dessert, aware of her gardening skills, Mr. Hartwell asked, "Rose, what do you suggest I do about my rhododendron bushes?"

"What's wrong with them, Simon?"

"They're wilting terribly," he lamented, refilling his coffee cup.

"Do you water them?" she asked, passing the cream.

"All the time."

"Are they located in the sun?"

He nodded.

"Aha!" she exclaimed. "That's the problem. Rhododendrons are like robbers. Just as robbers prefer the cover of darkness, so rhododendrons prefer shade."

They all laughed at her analogy.

"And, of course, it helps if the soil is acidic," she added.

In an exaggerated tone of helplessness Mr. Hartwell asked, "How about doing me a favor, Rose? Will you come over and take a look at them?"

Julie's mouth curved into a faint smile at her father's acting ability. She was seized with the impish desire to mention Roberto Diaz, his gardener. But she was so pleased to see him enjoying himself, she fought off the urge.

Eager to accept his offer, Mrs. Baxter replied, "What's a good time for you?"

Mr. Hartwell's response was swift and decisive. "I'll pick you up at ten tomorrow morning."

Turning to her son, she asked, "Do you mind if I go to Simon's tomorrow to look at his rhododendrons?"

"No, not at all," he replied with a conspiratorial wink at Julie.

When finally Ned arose to bring the supper date to an end, Mr. Hartwell looked genuinely disappointed. Then his face brightened. "How would all of you like to drive out to Rocky Point and do some ballroom dancing?" he suggested.

"Dad, I don't think—"

Before Julie could politely decline his invitation, Mrs. Baxter said enthusiastically, "That sounds like a wonderful idea!"

"I know you're going to love the place," her father said. "It's aptly named the Rosewood Ballroom."

His humor brought a blush to her face.

Mr. Hartwell insisted on paying the bill. Taking Mrs. Baxter by the arm, he led her out of the restaurant. The younger couple, astonished at the camaraderie of their parents, trailed behind.

From the moment they first arrived at Rosewood until the last musical flourish of the band, Mrs. Baxter and Mr. Hartwell never once strayed from the dance floor. Although Julie and Ned made several forays across the crowded room, neither their enthusiasm nor their endurance were a match for that of their parents. Soon they slumped down, exhausted, onto a bench, content to spend the rest of the evening watching the other two flitting endlessly back and forth in front of the bandstand.

Julie leaned over to Ned, saying, "I can't believe it. They look as if they could go on dancing all night."

"Wake me up when it's time to leave," he said, closing his eyes and pretending to sleep.

"They're behaving like old friends." She shook her head in disbelief.

"More like long-lost lovers," he replied, his mouth twisting wryly.

"Yes," she said, matching his smile with one of her own. "Congratulations!"

"For what?"

"Your plan to foist your mom off on my dad has worked superbly." Her eyes sparkled with laughter.

"Better than I ever could have imagined," he replied, squeezing her hand gratefully.

Chapter Ten

Ever since Julie could remember, she had wanted to spend a September at Paradise Cove. For her, that month always meant an end to the warm, lazy days of summer and the start of another hectic, arduous year at school or college.

Now she came to appreciate the town's finer qualities. With mild days and cool evenings, its weather was ideal for enjoying the sunlight hours and sleeping comfortably at night. After Labor Day weekend the bustling seaside community was transformed into a ghost town. The friendly young gate guards who had once inhabited the freshly painted sentry boxes at the entrances to the public beaches had deserted Paradise Cove for their autumnal haunts. Now the empty parking lots served only as landing fields for occasional gulls.

To her delight, Julie suddenly had the best beaches all to herself, and she took full advantage of her good fortune by indulging in her passion for walking. As she strolled along their sandy white stretches, she thought surely she'd come upon some of the common sights of summer. At any moment she expected to see an overweight father stagger out from behind a sand dune, burdened down with a brimming cooler and beach chairs. Following closely behind would be his harried wife, holding on anxiously to the hands of her eager youngsters. Or perhaps around the next bend Julie would stumble upon a gaggle of teenagers dozing beneath the noonday sun with their radios blaring. But such thoughts were merely memories from summers past. So, like a forbidden fruit never before tasted, Julie now savored the sweetness of her first September in Paradise Cove.

The subtle changes of the fall season captivated her. The singing of crickets, gathered around the base of the house, grew louder. The bolder among them even sought out the warmth of her cellar, where they serenaded her all night long. Mornings, over coffee, she would look out her kitchen window and behold the lawn proudly sporting a coat of heavy dew, which it wouldn't shed until the rising sun gave its permission. In October she felt a sense of exhilaration at bicycling through hails of falling leaves. Later she would experience that same thrill at the sound of their rustling about her ankles as she sauntered down the narrow woodland paths they carpeted.

Julie and Ned held to their agreement to date only on weekends. He was trying desperately to put the finishing touches on the final draft of his book. A severe case of writer's block was making his task more difficult than he had expected. Since the book's completion was so important to both of them, she gave him plenty of moral support and resigned herself to spending long hours alone.

Although she was thankful that she owned The Gull's Way, daily household expenses were taking a toll on her savings. Steadfastly refusing all offers of monetary help from her father, she began once again to give serious thought to her career plans. This time any job would have to be within a reasonable commuting distance of Paradise Cove.

One morning while she was out for a stroll around the edge of a salt marsh, she passed a group of students and teachers. To her surprise, one of them called her name.

Turning, she immediately recognized her childhood friend Sally Westlake, who still wore her hair with bangs. Her family, like Julie's, had summered for years in Paradise Cove. Mr. Westlake, a successful surgeon, had spared no cost in sending his daughter to the finest private schools and colleges around.

"What are you doing here at this time of year?" Sally asked.

"I live here all year now," Julie replied with the pride of a native.

"But I heard you were working in Washington," her friend said.

"I'm afraid I missed Paradise Cove so much I just had to return," Julie said with a laugh. Nodding toward the others, who were moving slowly off into the distance, she added, "Unless my eyes are deceiving me, you must be teaching."

"Yes," Sally replied in a voice noticeably lacking in enthusiasm. "I teach biology at the regional high school. I just had to have something to occupy my time when Ted was out of town on his business trips." As she raised her arm to check the time on her watch, Julie noticed her wedding band.

"So you finally caught the Greek god," Julie said in jest.

"Yes," Sally said with a blush.

Julie remembered Ted Nettles as a popular, fun-loving summer warrior who hung out at the yacht club, so handsome that his peers referred to him good-naturedly as the Greek god. Julie's friends had idolized him. By the end of each summer he had invariably left a string of broken hearts in his wake. Sally had been relentless in her pursuit of him.

"And what are you doing for work now?" Sally asked, putting an end to Julie's musing.

"I'm among the ranks of the unemployed."

"Didn't you major in government?"

Julie nodded.

"Why don't you think about doing some substitute teaching at the high school? After all, you were the best sailing instructor the yacht club ever had," Sally quipped. "Besides, the social-studies department is looking for qualified people to fill in. You can sign up at the superintendent's office." The band of students had disappeared from sight, and Sally again glanced nervously at her watch. "I've got to catch up with my juvenile delinquents before they turn this field trip into a wild party," she exclaimed. "It's been nice seeing you again."

"Likewise," Julie called after her.

"Don't forget to stop by the superintendent's office," Sally called back.

On her way into town on shopping errands Julie drove past the office of the superintendent of schools many times before getting up the courage to go inside and fill out an application.

To her surprise, a few days later she got a telephone call asking her to report for work at the high school on Monday. Early Monday morning she signed in at the principal's office and met briefly with the head of the social-studies department before setting out to find Room 121. Wandering past clusters of chattering teenagers gathered in front of pastel-colored lockers lining the corridors, she located it and went inside.

While she was giving the lesson plan on the desk a cursory inspection, students began drifting in, several of whom subjected her to a mischievous scrutiny. When the bell rang, she took a deep breath, closed the door, and turned to face the sea of youthful faces that made up her class in United States history.

From the lesson plan she chose those topics with which she felt most comfortable. Rather than lecture, she asked open-ended questions to draw the students out. Lively discussions ensued, and the tense feeling in the pit of her stomach eased. Her second class, a senior elective in international relations, went even more smoothly since the pupils were more mature and motivated. Before she realized it, the day had passed. Not only had she survived but she had enjoyed the experience immensely too. That afternoon she skipped down the granite steps of the building, eagerly looking forward to returning.

Ned was still struggling with writer's block, and progress on his book was at a standstill. Julie was so busy trying to lift his sagging spirits that she didn't mention her job. At a more propitious time she would surprise him.

Often she found herself looking back with amusement upon her first encounter with Ned.

She marveled at the mysterious process of love that transformed her initial disdain for him into deep affection. Now, at restaurants, over empty coffee cups, their glances would meet, bringing knowing smiles to both their faces. The mere clasp of their hands produced electricity.

Ned avoided the subject of marriage, and Julie knew the reason. He had given up a well-paying job as a newspaper columnist for the Spartan simplicity of a cabin where he was determined to earn a living as a free-lance writer. Times were difficult for him. Although his father, a successful salesman, had left his mother well-off, Ned, like Julie, wouldn't accept any help from his parent. His pride and fierce independence made him all the more desirable to her.

On a warm, Indian-summer Saturday in late October, Julie and Ned took advantage of the fine weather to go sailing. For sentimental reasons, they stopped at Braddock's Island. Upon landing there, they stood silently, holding hands, on the very spot where earlier they had exchanged harsh words. "How does it feel to return to the scene of the crime?" she asked, finally breaking the spell.

"Wonderful," he said, smiling at her and pretending to push their sailboat back into the open water without its passengers.

"Don't you dare," she replied, playfully pointing a finger at him.

"I want to spend the rest of my life on this island with you," he whispered, reaching over and drawing her to him.

"In that case you'll never get your book finished," she said teasingly, pulling his face down to meet hers. "I'd be too distracting."

"I'm beginning to think I'd rather make history than write about it," he replied, kissing her gently.

Later, seated cozily on a blanket, they shared sandwiches and coffee, which she had packed for the occasion. Propped up on an elbow, he was staring pensively out to sea. "Why are you looking so glum?" she asked, studying him over the rim of a Styrofoam cup.

"Because right now all I have to offer you is a future of genteel poverty."

"Sounds good enough to me," she replied, sliding over and leaning back against his chest.

"I want my wife to have the best," he mused aloud, slipping an arm around her waist.

She snuggled up to him. "I just happen to think you *are* the best," she murmured.

"You're too easy to please. What if I don't make it as a writer of nonfiction books?"

"I have great confidence in your ability," she replied, turning her face toward him invitingly. "If you weren't so macho, I'd suggest you let me support you until you become established as a writer," she added jokingly.

His eyes widened in curiosity. "And just how do you propose to do that?"

"I've started working part-time as a substitute teacher at Concordia Regional High," she said.

"You're kidding." The surprise on his face matched that in his words.

"Why do you find that so hard to believe?"

"I just wish I could have had a teacher like you when I went to school," he whispered, kissing the hollow of her neck. "I would have refused to graduate."

For the rest of the afternoon they remained on the island, savoring the mild weather, the tranquility, and each other's company. Only when a strong sea breeze sprang up, churning the waters of the bay, did they arise and reluctantly climb back into the sailboat. Pushing off from shore, they set sail for The Gull's Way.

Julie soon discovered that even the cold months at Paradise Cove held a certain charm. In November an early snowstorm brushed the coastal community, dumping a foot of snow before blowing out to sea. Since school was canceled, she donned her winter clothes and boots to go out for a walk.

In her delight at the vagaries of the New England weather, she rambled down narrow seaside lanes, leaving footprints on nature's pristine carpet. Only lonely, tightly shuttered cottages bore silent witness to her wanderings. The lobster pots, neatly stacked on the town pier, seemed almost edible with their frosting of white snow. Out on the frigid waters of the bay, whitecaps danced as if mocking the timidity of boats, long since hauled up to the safety of dry land. Even as she stood on Wyman's Wharf, the whistling wind whispered words of wisdom to her: *To enjoy a summer at Paradise Cove, you must first endure its winter.* Retracing her steps homeward, she smiled, for she now realized just what it meant to be a year-round resident of Paradise Cove.

Despite Julie's short temper, a personal fault that she readily admitted to her students, she showed enthusiasm, patience, and genuine concern for their well-being. They in turn responded positively to her teaching style, and soon even the English and French departments were requesting her services as a substitute teacher. When one of the senior members of the social-studies staff underwent surgery and was unable to return to school, Julie was elated at being offered a full-time position as her replacement.

One Saturday afternoon she and Ned were sharing a pizza at Mama Leone's when some high-school girls swarmed around their table.

They peppered her with questions about the results of a recent exam they had taken in her history class. Addressing each one by name, she allayed their fears and chatted amiably. Ned looked on in admiration.

Later, outside, as they were crossing the street to his van, she caught him chuckling. "Would you mind sharing your private joke with me?" she said in good humor.

"I'm amazed that you have so much patience with those giggling adolescents," he replied, gesturing at the pizzeria, "and so little with a serious fellow like me."

"That's because you're a nasty, cynical old adult and they're nice, open-minded young people." She tried to look serious.

"I may be old, but I'm sure I could easily pass one of your exams," he said, hurling a roguish challenge at her.

"Just for that, I'm going to give you a quiz right now," she replied, stopping on the sidewalk and turning to face him.

"Oh?"

"Yes, the osculation test," she said, standing on tiptoes and touching her lips to his.

He wasted no time in responding with a kiss that for her was as refreshing and titillating as any summer breeze that ever had swept across Paradise Cove. "How'd I do, teach?" he asked, coaxing his lips away from hers.

"A-plus," she murmured breathlessly.

Just as she was reaching up for another kiss, a chorus of young voices called from across the street, "Does your mother know where you are, Miss Hartwell?"

Blushing, she waved to them before replying, "No, but my father does." Meanwhile Ned burst out into laughter.

The following day, Julie came across unexpected news about Roger Whitman as she was leafing through the paper in search of news items to use with her students in class discussion. A bold headline on one of the pages announced: LIBERAL REFORMER UPSETS SENATOR WHITMAN.

> *Senator Roger Whitman,* she read, *once considered a rising star within his party and a possible presidential candidate, suffered a stunning defeat by liberal reformer Peter Anderson. The incumbent's links to certain defense companies became the dominant theme of the campaign. Mr. Anderson kept hammering away at Senator Whitman's poor judgment in accepting perks from one company in particular—Acme Electronics. Senator Whitman was noncommittal about his future plans.*

A feeling of sweet revenge welled up within her. "The wheels of justice grind slowly, but they grind exceedingly fine," she said softly.

Chapter Eleven

As a fine stream of warm water sprayed over Julie from the brass shower head above, she found herself singing. She could hardly remember a time when she felt so happy. All the pieces of the grand puzzle of her life now were falling neatly into place.

Each day at school made her all the more certain that teaching was her calling in life. That afternoon the junior-class officers had asked her to serve as their adviser for the next school year, an honor she accepted with great humility.

Eager to become a master teacher, Julie had decided to get an advanced degree in education, so she had enrolled in evening classes at the state university. On Mondays and Wednesdays she would leave for work at seven o'clock in the morning and not return home from college until eleven at night. But she didn't complain, for the courses were exciting and informative.

Sometimes, on weekend dates, she would ask Ned to drop her off early so she could study for an exam in her course "The Reluctant Learner." Before allowing her to leave his warm embrace, he would say teasingly, "I can assure you that in a class with a teacher as beautiful as you, there can be no reluctant learners."

The cloud of depression that had hung over her father had lifted. She was pleased to see him positive and jovial once again. Earlier that week he had surprised her with a telephone call. Since he had been out of town on business, Julie at first had feared something might have happened to him. But to her relief, he sounded as though he were in excellent spirits. The purpose of his call was to invite her and Ned to join him for dinner at the Starboard Galley on Saturday. Something important had happened that he wanted to share with them in person. Despite her cajoling, all he would say was that he would pick them up at The Gull's Way promptly at six on Saturday. So now Julie resigned herself to waiting until tomorrow to learn more about this matter of earthshaking importance.

Ned had cast off the shackles of writer's block that had fettered his literary talent for so long and, in a spontaneous outburst of creativity, had finished the book. In his exuberance he had asked Julie to celebrate that feat with him by driving up to Boston for supper and an evening concert.

Only the feeling of his arms around her could be more enjoyable than the soothing warmth of the water now cascading down upon her, she thought. Realizing that he'd be arriving soon to pick her up, she toweled herself off and reached for her satin robe. Returning to the bedroom, she sat down in front of the mirror and used the blow dryer on her tawny hair. As she was brushing it out, an eerie feeling that she was being watched sent a shudder through her. Putting down her brush, she slowly turned around.

To her dismay, Roger Whitman was lounging on her bed with his head propped against the headboard and his arms folded casually across his chest. His suit coat and vest were set neatly on a nearby chair, beneath which lay his polished shoes. A leer revealed just how much he was enjoying the sight of her primping. "What are you doing here?" she gasped.

"I was hoping I might get to witness the unveiling," he replied, his eyes gleaming.

"You're sickening," she snapped, rising to confront him.

"You shouldn't leave your doors unlocked," he said, unperturbed by the hostile reception, "unless, of course, you're expecting the man of your dreams."

His attempt at humor fell on deaf ears. "You scared me out of my wits," she said angrily.

His eyes traveled over her slowly. "I've come to take you back to Washington with me," he announced.

His arrogance drew her swift response. "I can't believe you'd dare show your face here after—"

"The accident was most unfortunate," he said smoothly, as if reading her mind. "I'm sorry about it."

"Sorry." She let out a scornful laugh. "You left me there to die, and all you can say is that you're sorry!"

"I made a mistake in judgment." The confidence in his voice gave way to uncertainty. He got up and sauntered to the liquor cabinet in the adjoining room. "I need a drink."

She followed closely, upset at the way he made himself so comfortable in her home.

"When the car landed at the edge of the brook, I was shaken up," he said, pouring himself a generous drink. "But I managed to reach over and feel your pulse. I couldn't find it." As he spoke, he clenched his glass so tightly she thought it might shatter in his hand.

"So you decided to flee the scene as quickly as possible to save your precious political neck." All her pent-up anger over his cowardly actions the night of the accident now came gushing forth.

"Believe me, I'd never have left you, but I thought you were—" He stammered, breaking off contact with her accusing eyes.

"Dead," she filled in the missing word, glaring at him.

"Yes," he mumbled, stroking his mustache, "and I was certain nothing I could do would bring you back to life."

"I hope you're a better politician than you are a paramedic," she said sarcastically.

He flinched at the venom in her words.

"Obviously you didn't want my death to elicit difficult questions that a distinguished senator like you would have to answer," she went on. "That would be embarrassing—particularly during a reelection campaign."

He raised the glass to his lips and drained the contents. "You don't know the living hell I've been through," he said.

"I can just imagine." The corners of her mouth curled in derision.

"When I learned you were alive, I wept for joy. I tried to telephone you, but you hung up."

"What did you expect me to do?" she retorted. "Give you a medal for heroism?"

"I'm not proud of what I did. But I'm here to make it up to you." He began pacing back and forth. "I'd have come sooner but I was involved in a tough reelection campaign, which unfortunately I lost." His eyes were pleading for her sympathy.

There was none as she replied matter-of-factly, "So I read in the newspaper."

"It was a bitter race," he said. "My opponent was a master at innuendo and accusation. Throughout the campaign he did nothing but sling mud."

His self-righteous manner infuriated her, and she wanted to lash out at him, citing his personal greed in seizing all kinds of perks and PAC money from Acme Electronics. Only a lingering fear of the consequences such an outburst might have on her father's job prevented her. So she bit her tongue, saying, "Apparently some of it must have stuck."

He stiffened. "I don't blame you for feeling the way you do. Anyway, I've put my political defeat behind me. But you—" He paused, his eyes narrowing in another lengthy appraisal of her. "I couldn't forget you so easily. Without you, my life's been as empty as this glass." He set it down forcefully to emphasize his point.

"How ironic," she mocked. "Mine's been brimming with happiness."

Disregarding her sarcasm, he said imploringly, "I need you."

"I certainly don't feel the same way about you," she told him.

He refused to accept her rejection. "For the first time in my life, I'm completely free—free of Tracy and the burden of any political responsibility."

Her skin prickled at his mention of Tracy, and she shook her head, more in sadness than anger. "Why couldn't you just have stayed away from me?" she asked.

"Stay away?" he asked in disbelief. "Never! We can spend a lifetime together. With you by my side, I can make another bid for public office. And I know I can be a winner again."

Her thoughts went back to their first meeting at The Gull's Way. At the time his eloquence had struck a responsive chord within her. But, like Roger himself, those words turned out to be empty and misleading. Any positive feelings she might have held for him had vanished the night of the accident. "Why don't you do both the country and me a favor and forget about running for political office again?" she said icily.

Although his eyes hardened, he continued to smile as he reminded her, "I may have lost the election, but I can still help your father get the promotion he wants."

This time she refused to succumb to his political blackmail. "I'd appreciate your leaving my father out of this conversation! Any problem is between you and me."

"As far as you're concerned, I didn't come all the way here to take no for an answer," he said, for the first time showing his displeasure with her. "Let's stop playing games. You want me as much as I want you."

He moved toward her—so close she could smell the odor of liquor on his breath. She now realized he had been drinking heavily before his arrival at The Gull's Way. *How else could he have gotten up the courage to show up here?* she thought.

"That's not true." She pulled her robe more tightly around her and stepped back from him, but he grabbed her by the arm and pulled her roughly to him, forcing his lips on hers.

"Let go of me!" she demanded, tearing her face from his.

"Now tell me you didn't enjoy that," he said, tightening his grip on her.

At that moment, the back door slammed and Ned called out, "Jewel, where are you?" A second later he was in the room.

The sight of her in Roger's arms brought him to an abrupt halt. "Pardon me!" he said sarcastically, the color draining from his face. "I didn't know I was interrupting such an intimate moment."

Roger relaxed his grip, and Julie seized the opportunity to pull herself free of him. Both angry and embarrassed, she struggled to remain calm, saying, "Ned, I can explain this."

Casting a withering glance at her, he replied, "I just bet you can."

Emboldened by their sharp exchange of

words, Roger stepped forward to challenge his younger rival. "I can see that when the cat's away, the mice will play," he said. "Today I've returned to claim what's rightfully mine."

"You're welcome to her," Ned muttered.

Julie didn't know what hurt more—the scorn in Ned's words or the pain in his eyes. Finally he turned to her, saying, "I'm amazed that you could have anything to do with him after the way he treated you the night of the accident."

Roger became flustered and cast a wary glance at her.

Reacting to his uneasiness, Ned taunted, "Oh, don't worry, she's been true to you. She hasn't shared your secret with me."

Roger nervously tugged at the corners of his mustache. "I have no idea what you're talking about," he protested.

"I know you were at the wheel of her car that night," Ned said reproachfully to the squirming politician.

"I'm afraid you're sadly mistaken," Roger stammered.

"I saw you crossing the road." Ned smiled disdainfully. "I could tell it was you by the yellow stripe running down your back."

"You should teach your friend some manners," Roger told Julie, his nostrils flaring in anger. "If you don't, I will."

At that threat she saw Ned's body tense up

and his hands clench into fists. As Ned moved forward menacingly, Roger retreated behind Julie. "Ned, stop it," she demanded.

"Even now you'd protect him." Ned stared down at her, shaking his head in disillusion.

She took hold of his arm. "Let me explain."

"That won't be necessary." He tore himself from her grasp. "You both deserve each other and I apologize for spoiling your reunion." He turned and strode out of the house.

Julie ran after him, but by the time she got outside, Ned was already in his van. As she ran toward him, he turned on the engine and drove off, burning rubber in his haste to put as much distance as possible between them.

"What do I do now?" she cried out, throwing her hands in the air. For a moment she stood in the driveway, frozen by despair. Gradually the despair gave way to resolve.

Whirling around, she reentered the house and went directly to the hall closet, from which she took out her father's hunting rifle and some shells. With the loaded gun firmly tucked under her arm, she marched out to the sun porch where Roger, coatless and shoeless, had wandered. "Are you still here?" she asked tersely.

With another drink in his hand, he was lounging against the arm of a sofa and looking out at the panoramic view of the bay. "Yes, and I want you to gather all your clothes together," he told her officiously. "I have no intention of returning to Washington without you."

As he turned to face her, he recoiled at finding himself looking down the barrel of the rifle. "For heaven's sake, put that thing away before it goes off," he demanded, moving toward her with extreme caution.

"Stay away from me, or I swear I'll shoot," she warned, brandishing the weapon.

"Whatever you say," he said, gesturing with his hands and stepping back discreetly. "Just don't do anything reckless."

Meanwhile she edged over to the telephone extension. Keeping an alert eye on him, she dialed with her free hand. After a long pause, during which her index finger curled around the trigger, she said, "Operator, this is an emergency. Get me the police!"

"What are you doing?" he asked.

"I'm going to tell the police that a certain ex-senator broke into my home and I shot him in self-defense," she replied matter-of-factly, resting the receiver in the hollow of her neck.

"Please don't do anything you'll regret," he said, so agitated he was waving his arms wildly.

"I'll have no regrets. On the contrary, I'll enjoy it." Again she motioned him back with the barrel of the weapon before adding, "I can see the newspaper headlines now: *Oversexed, Overpaid Ex-Congressman Mortally Wounded in Former Aide's Home—and Not by One of Cupid's Arrows!* That item should cause quite a stir in the senate chamber, shouldn't it?"

"Have you gone mad?" he exclaimed.

"I had to be out of my mind ever to have believed in you," she replied with a scowl. "Now take off your clothes."

"What?" he asked in disbelief.

"You heard me."

"But—" As she raised the rifle, he knew resistance was futile and slowly removed his tie.

He was toying with the buttons on his shirt and she grew impatient, saying, "Hurry up and take it off."

Again he obeyed with reluctance and started folding it as if he were wrapping a Christmas present.

"Just put the shirt on the floor," she said in exasperation.

With a grimace, he set it down.

"Now drop your trousers."

"See here," he retorted, glaring at her with a newfound defiance. "I refuse to—"

She poked him with the barrel of the rifle, cutting short his speech.

Shivering at the touch of the cold steel on his bare skin, he danced back a few steps. "Don't do that," he implored, quickly loosening his belt.

His pants fell to the floor. Staring at his spindly legs and bony knees, she needed all her self-control not to burst out laughing at the incongruity of the once influential politician now shivering before her in his boxer shorts and socks. "I'm sure we can work out some kind of compromise," he said, jarring her out of her musing.

"It's too late for compromises," she replied frostily.

"But there's a simple solution." His tone was one of desperation.

"Yes, and I have it right here," she answered, stroking the barrel of the rifle.

"I'll disappear from your life forever," he entreated. "You'll never hear from me again."

"Is that a promise?" she asked.

"Yes, I swear," he exclaimed, raising his hand to show his willingness to take an oath upon it.

Julie still was holding the receiver to her ear, but the frightened Roger didn't know she had depressed the button and faked her conversation with the operator. Now she dropped the receiver onto its cradle with such a bang that for an instant he thought the gun had gone off and mortally wounded him. "What are you waiting for?" she asked.

Realizing he wasn't hurt, he said, "Surely you're not going to send me out there in my undershorts? I'll catch my death of cold."

Her expression was impassive, for her thoughts were on Tracy.

At the sound of her cocking the rifle, he started backing slowly toward the door. "Please don't shoot, I'm going." He was pleading with his hands raised over his head. "You'll never see or hear from me again."

"Hallelujah," she muttered.

With lightninglike speed he turned and hurled himself against the storm door—so forcefully that he tumbled down the steps to the ground outside. Scrambling to his feet, he raced across the yard. Just to prove she meant business, Julie opened the door and fired a warning shot in the air over the water. At the sound, Roger somersaulted over a hedge and rolled several feet across the lawn before resuming his headlong flight down the road.

If Roger's sudden appearance at The Gull's Way had shocked her, Ned's hasty retreat had angered her. How dare he jump to conclusions and go running off like a jealous schoolboy! The more she thought about his actions, the more incensed she became. Such immaturity on his part was inexcusable. If he didn't trust her, how could she ever hope to build a future with him? Better that she should find out about that character flaw now than later, she fumed.

The evening passed without a word from him, and Saturday Julie found herself moping around the house, her resentment simmering. To lift her spirits, she was just about to go for a walk along the shoreline when she realized her father would be arriving to take her and Ned out to dinner. "Impossible!" she muttered. "I wouldn't be seen dead with him."

She hurried over to the telephone and called her father, hoping to cancel their meeting. There was no answer. Glancing at the wall clock, she murmured, "He's already on his way here."

The last thing she needed was to explain to her father what had gone wrong between Ned and herself. But now she had to resign herself to doing exactly that.

It wasn't long before she heard a car pulling into the driveway. Soon the front door opened and her father escorted Mrs. Baxter across the threshold. Before Julie could recover from her surprise at the sight of them, he blurted out, "Rose and I are going to be married!"

"Oh, Simon!" Mrs. Baxter chided. "You were supposed to wait until Ned arrives before making the announcement."

"I'm so happy, I want to shout it from the rooftop," he said.

Julie's knees buckled, and she slumped down into an armchair. The events of the previous night had sapped her strength and now this latest bit of news—however pleasant—toppled her.

Surprised at her reaction, Mrs. Baxter asked, "You don't approve?"

"Of course I do!" Julie assured her. "I'm delighted and wish you all the happiness in the world."

"Then, what's bothering you?" her father asked.

"It's Ned," she confessed.

Mrs. Baxter's ears perked up in alarm. "Where's my son? Has something happened to him?"

"No, it's—" Julie stammered. "It's just that we're no longer seeing each other."

"But why?" her father asked in disbelief.

She searched for a plausible explanation. "Because he thinks I don't love him," she finally blurted out.

"What could possibly have given him such a silly idea?" he asked.

Taking a deep breath, Julie replied, "Roger Whitman barged in here last night."

The mention of that name brought a scowl to his face. "What did he want?"

"He insisted that I return to Washington and marry him." As she spoke, she turned her eyes away from her father. "Ned became furious and drove off. I haven't seen or heard from him since."

"Under the circumstances I could hardly blame him," Mrs. Baxter remarked drily.

Mr. Hartwell rallied to his daughter's defense, saying, "Rose, I can assure you there's nothing between Julie and Roger. I'd just like to get my hands on him."

"He's the least of my worries now," Julie replied with a heavy sigh.

"What do you mean?" Her father's face clouded over with uneasiness.

"With the help of your hunting rifle, I got rid of him for good."

Her words aroused his worst fears. "I hope you didn't shoot him," he said, his mouth agape.

"Oh, Dad!" she replied in exasperation. "Of course not."

In a rare display of self-control, Mrs. Baxter had been standing all this time, trying to make some sense out of their conversation. With a perplexed expression she finally asked, "Who's Roger?"

"An ex-senator who's always had a hankering for my daughter. Fortunately she's had the good sense to ignore him and seek out somebody more worthy of her—someone like Ned."

His emphasis on the last word made Julie uneasy. It was more than just a clarification for his wife-to-be. It was his way of showing disapproval at her breakup with Ned.

"My son can be stubborn," Mrs. Baxter said. "It's a trait I'm afraid he's inherited from me."

"He's not as stubborn as Julie, I assure you." Now Mr. Hartwell openly scolded his daughter.

Although a crimson flush stained Julie's cheeks, she said nothing. She knew her father was right.

He turned to Mrs. Baxter, complaining, "Rose, I just wish we could have made our announcement under happier circumstances."

"Now, let's not become morbid, Simon," she replied, taking his hand. "We can't run our children's lives—believe me, nobody knows that better than I—but we certainly can control our own. You and I will go to the Starboard Galley and enjoy ourselves."

"Yes, of course," he answered, his voice lacking its earlier enthusiasm, "but first I want to tell Julie that I'm taking early retirement from Acme Electronics."

His words jarred her out of her silence. "But what about your promotion?" she gasped.

"It really doesn't matter anymore. There's something else you should know too." He wiped a bead of perspiration from his forehead. "I've been working undercover for the Attorney General's office in their investigation of political corruption at Acme. Roger Whitman's finally going to get his comeuppance. That's for sure."

That revelation so shocked Julie that words failed her.

"Ned helped me to contact the proper Federal officials." He paused as if to measure her reaction to his mention of the young man's name. "That's really why he came to see me on that visit that upset you so much."

"I can't believe all this happened," Julie said, shaking her head.

"It's true, all right," Mrs. Baxter chimed in. "After his final meeting with the law officials in Washington, he came out to California and proposed to me." She turned and rewarded him with a smile. "He called you while we were enroute. We wanted to share the news of our impending marriage with you and Ned over dinner at the Starboard Galley."

"But that just wasn't to be," Mr. Hartwell said with a sigh of resignation.

Moved by his somber look and cheerless words, Julie burst out, "I think it's great that the two of you are getting married! I wish you lots of happiness in the future."

As the couple moved toward the door, Mrs. Baxter turned around, saying, "It's not my intention to meddle in your business, Julie, but I do know one thing for certain: Ned cares for you very deeply. It would be a shame to allow a foolish misunderstanding to destroy your love for each other. Here's my key to his cabin, in case you change your mind."

Her father peered at her over his bifocals. Although he said nothing, the message in his eyes was loud and clear. As the door closed behind them, Julie played with the key, more confused than ever about her next course of action.

Her father's sadness at her breakup with Ned—so obvious in his words and gestures—hurt her. Nor did Mrs. Baxter's advice go unheeded. Yes, Ned loved her, she knew that. And she, too, was in love with him. Why was foolish pride always getting in their way?

As she stared down at the key lying in the palm of her hand, a faint smile crossed her lips. Ned and she had come so far together. Why give it all up so easily? Not only did she hold the key to his cabin but—more important—she had the one to his heart.

With renewed vigor she arose and hastened out to her car. The closer her Porsche moved to the cabin, the more certain she felt that she had made the right decision. When she pulled to a stop amid the towering conifers, Ned's van was nowhere in sight. *He's worth waiting for,* she thought, climbing out.

For a long time she stood and inhaled the salt air and pine scent, which mingled to form a balm for her bruised ego. Finally she opened the door with her key and went inside. The neat and cozy interior drew a smile from her. Settling down onto the nearest chair, she awaited Ned's arrival.

Julie didn't know how long she had been dozing, but the sound of Ned's van moving up the dirt road awoke her. Soon footsteps echoed on the graveled walkway. She took a deep breath and crossed her fingers.

The door swung open, and in he strode. Coming to a sudden stop in the center of the room, he whirled around, exclaiming, "How'd you get in here?"

Instinctively she arose and went to the door. "Your mother gave me her key," she replied.

"So you've even corrupted her," he said accusingly.

Julie rushed to the defense of the other woman, saying, "She's a fine person who'd never do anything to hurt you."

"The last thing I need from you is a lecture on my mother's positive personal qualities," he said, moving slowly toward her.

As he loomed over her, she held her ground, her body and outspread arms blocking his way. "I'm going to stand here until you agree to hear me out," she said, looking up at the taut line of his mouth.

"Right now you're really testing my patience," he replied, viewing her threat with amused irritation.

"You're the best thing that's ever happened to me, and I'm not going to lose you again," she blurted out.

Her resolute tone brought him up short, but he shook off its effects. "Save that sweet talk for Roger."

"Now, wait just a minute!" she demanded in righteous indignation. "I know what you saw at The Gull's Way didn't look right, but I'm not going to let you send me on a guilt trip. You're the one who ought to be ashamed. The way you ran out was immature, to say the least. Had you given me a chance to explain, you'd have learned that he broke into my house."

That admission brought a crimson flush to his face. Softening his tone, he asked, "Why'd he do a dumb thing like that?"

Swallowing hard, she replied, "To apologize for his cowardly actions the night of the accident and to take me back to Washington as his wife."

He stood in stony silence, only the muscles in his jaw betraying the impact of her candor.

"Now if you'll permit me," she said in a low, composed voice, "I'd like to tell you exactly what happened on that day you found me unconscious in my car."

Settling onto the sofa, he gave his consent with a nod.

"That afternoon Roger telephoned me from the airport, demanding that I have supper with him for old times' sake. Since I had quit my job leaving only a letter to explain my reasons, I thought I should at least go and tell him to his face just how I felt about him." She shifted her weight and leaned back against the door. "I quickly realized I had made a colossal blunder by agreeing to see him, and I couldn't get through the meal fast enough to get him back for his flight."

Ned stirred uneasily on the sofa.

"Outside the restaurant he insisted on driving my Porsche to the airport," she went on. "Although he had been drinking and I had some qualms, I was so eager to get the ordeal over with, I stupidly gave him my car keys."

"So he *was* driving, after all?" he murmured.

"Yes," she replied sheepishly. "When I refused to return to Washington with him, his temper flared. The angrier he became, the faster he drove. On Ridge Road at the curve above Jones Brook, the car veered out of control and rolled down the embankment. The next thing I remember—thanks to you—is waking up in the hospital."

He broke the long silence that followed. "Why didn't you tell the police he was driving?"

"Because I wanted to protect my father," she replied, her voice trailing off to a whisper.

"So you weren't covering up for Roger after all," he muttered, enlightenment dawning. "You were only trying to protect your father."

She nodded in agreement as he arose and moved toward her.

"What a fool I've been!" he said apologetically, his arms reaching out for her.

"Don't put all the blame on yourself," she

replied, eagerly allowing them to encircle her. "I should have trusted you enough to tell you the whole story."

"When I saw you together, I thought you were in love with him." Tenderly he pushed away wisps of hair that denied him a full view of her smiling face.

"Perish the thought," she replied, gazing up at him. "With the help of my father's hunting rifle, I sent him running—and not for public office."

He was grinning, and to Julie, his smile was like the reemergence of the sun after a severe noonday thunderstorm.

"When I saw you in his arms, I suddenly became so jealous and insecure," he confessed. "I just had to get away."

"So where have you been all day?"

"I ended up driving all the way to New York City last night, to see my literary agent and try to clear my head. At least while I was there I got some good news," he said, his eyes lighting up with that familiar twinkle. "My book's been accepted for publication, and I've gotten a generous advance."

"Oh, Ned, I'm so proud of you!" She threw her arms around him and kissed him.

He held her close, nestling his cheek against hers. "I love you so much," he whispered. "I'm sorry I acted like such a jerk last night. I did a lot of thinking while I was driving, and, down deep, I knew you would never betray me. And then when I came back and found you here, I was so ashamed of myself that I started acting like a jerk all over again—" His voice broke off as another thought hit him. "You said my mother gave you the key. I forgot all about dinner tonight."

"Don't worry about that. She and my dad went off to celebrate on their own." Julie pulled away and looked up at Ned, her smile lighting her face. "You'll be interested to know that they're getting married."

"You're kidding!" His eyes widened in astonishment.

"No," she said enthusiastically. "After their marriage, they'll live in his house. He's leaving Acme Electronics."

"So he's decided to take an early retirement?" he asked, his face taking on a more solemn expression.

"Yes." Her arms tightened around him. "Thanks to you, he's leaving that den of corruption with his character and integrity intact."

"I'm sure my mother will keep him busy." He grimaced in good humor.

"Naughty," she chastised him, running a finger across his lips. "She's a wonderful woman."

"Yes, just like you," he murmured. He raised an eyebrow mischievously. "Do you think our parents will object to a double wedding?" he asked.

"I think they'd love it," she whispered, offering her lips for another kiss.